Stories from
THE
BLUE ROAD

Stories from
THE
BLUE ROAD

by Emily Crofford

pictures C.A. Nobens

Carolrhoda Books, Inc. • Minneapolis

LIBRARY OF CONGRESS CATALOGING IN PUBLICATION DATA

Crofford, Emily.
    Stories from the Blue Road.

    Summary: Five episodes in the life of a family
living on an Arkansas cotton plantation during the
Depression.
    [1. Farm life—Fiction. 2. Family life—Fiction]
I. Nobens, C.A., ill. II. Title.
PZ7.C873St   [Fic]   81-21229
ISBN 0-87614-189-0   AACR2

1 2 3 4 5 6 7 8 9 10 88 87 86 85 84 83 82

To Mother and Daddy,
and to Bill, Cliff, Bettye, Martha,
Zola, Ronald—and Otis

Contents

Stories from
THE
BLUE ROAD

Every Body
Should
Have a Name

Bill didn't mean to name the runt pig. "It just sneaked into my head," he explained, and rubbed the end of his nose. He did that when he was about to be stubborn. He had a short nose anyway, and Mother said she was afraid he would erase it altogether.

"You're going to get into bad trouble," I said. It was all right for Mrs. Gruntling to have a name because she was our brood sow. We would keep her always, the same as we would Dolly, the cow we had gotten not long after we had moved to Arkansas. We were never to name the calves and pigs, though, because we would either butcher them or sell them.

Bill and I were picking bugs off the potato leaves, laying them on a plank, and squashing them with a stick before they could crawl away. Bill didn't like that job—he was too tender-hearted—but Mother said we had to do it or our late potatoes would get sick. Our little brother Correy, who was going on four, was supposed to be helping us, but mostly he was a nuisance. He had put his bugs in a jar and dumped them all back out.

"What kind of name is Otis for a pig, anyway?" I asked. "Why don't you just un-name him. He won't know any difference."

Correy didn't seem to be paying any attention to us, and Bill and I forgot that he heard everything.

"He knows his name is Otis," Bill said. "I named him when he was a suckling."

"You kept it a secret all this time?"

Bill nodded.

"You're sure? You didn't even tell LeRoy?" I had never heard of not telling at least one person a secret.

"No."

Bill wouldn't have told me, I thought, if I hadn't overheard him talking to Otis. I looked sternly at him and said in my Mother-voice, "Don't you remember Prince George?"

"Just plain George," he said.

We worked on in silence, both of us picturing the April morning Daddy had called for us to come to the barn to see Dolly's new calf, the first since we had bought her. Beaming, Daddy had stood rubbing Dolly's back. Bill and Correy and I had been too interested in the calf to pay attention to Dolly. Wobbling on his skinny legs, the calf was exploring the stall. As if he had suddenly discovered strange creatures in a big, exciting world, he stopped and stared at us.

"Hello, big-eyed George," Bill said to him.

"Prince George," I almost shouted. "It's perfect. Prince George!"

Daddy, still smiling, shook his head. "Sorry, Meg and Bill. You can't name him. Don't get friendly with him at all."

We had known why, but winter had seemed vague and far away, so every now and then Bill and I had slipped out to the barn and brushed Prince George.

Bill had thrown up over and over the day Daddy and some other men butchered the calf. And as meat-hungry as we had been, neither of us had been able to eat the veal.

Daddy had taken the blame himself that time, said he had failed to make us understand.

When the pigs had been born four months ago, he had made sure we understood. "You are not to name any of them," he had told us sternly.

Bill stopped squashing potato bugs. Gazing off over the cotton and corn fields, he said, "I know what Daddy told us."

"And you're still not going to un-name the runt pig?"

"I can't," he said. "Besides, every body ..."

I jumped up and kicked dirt on his legs. "Don't say it! Just don't say it, Bill Weston!"

He calmly brushed off the dirt, which aggravated me even more.

"I hope you're going to enjoy hanging by your toes from a barn rafter," I said. "Because that's what Daddy's going to do to you when he finds out you named that pig."

"He won't find out," Bill said. "I'm going to tell him."

"When?"

"Tonight. At the right time."

He didn't tell Daddy when he first came in from picking cotton. Daddy's shoulders were stooped then, and tired lines drew down the corners of his mouth. That was never a good time to talk to him. Bill didn't tell him at supper either. Daddy had begun to relax and get in a good mood, and Bill didn't want to spoil it.

We thought supper was over, but Mother had a surprise. She brought in a blackberry cobbler with the juice still bubbling around the dumpling islands.

"Ah," Daddy said.

We were all quiet while we took the first sweet-tart bites. Correy fidgeted and gave a little cough. I knew he figured he had finally gotten his chance; he was going to say something.

He looked from Daddy to Bill. "When . . ."

Suddenly I knew what he was about to ask. I butted in. "Your tongue is purple, Correy."

Correy stuck his tongue out and crossed his eyes to look down at it. We all laughed at him. Correy laughed too and took a drink of milk. I thought I had sidetracked him, but I hadn't.

"Bill's got something to tell you, Daddy," he said.

I glanced sharply at Bill, thinking he might grab Correy and strangle him. I should have known better. Bill was always calmest when he seemed to be in a hope-less predicament. He didn't look upset at all; his expression hadn't even changed.

"Well, what is it you want to tell me, Son?" Daddy asked Bill.

Bill pointed to his mouth because he had a piece of blackberry cobbler in it. After he swallowed it, he said, "I was going to tell you Correy helped gather the eggs. He didn't break a one."

It worked. Correy held out his hand. "See where the hen pecked me." He forgot about Otis.

"When?" I asked Bill later when Daddy was sitting in the rocking chair reading a newspaper and beginning to nod.

"At the right time."

"Let's go out on the porch," Daddy said. "Maybe the air will wake me up. It's too early to go to bed."

We went out on the front porch where a breeze stirred the hot first-of-September night. Daddy settled down in his chair and Mother in hers, and that's when Bill decided to tell him. In the moonlight I could see his bare feet. They were planted wide apart, the position they took when he had to tell something hard. The first time I had noticed that had been on the day he had gotten in trouble at school and had to go to the principal's office. I had promised not to tell Mother and Daddy, but Bill had gone right home and told them himself.

"Daddy," Bill said, "I didn't mean to name the runt pig. It just sneaked into my head."

Daddy didn't say a word.

"I named him Otis. He looks like a boy in my class named Otis."

Daddy still didn't say anything and I could see Bill's toes curling under.

"Every body should have a name," Bill said.

I closed my eyes and gritted my teeth. That drove me crazy. Over and over I had kindly explained to Bill that everybody was one word and that it only meant

people. Finally he had said, "In Mother's dictionary body is under B and every is under E."

It had turned out that he was right about Mother's old Webster. It didn't have everybody in it, not as one word anyway. I had argued then that in the big, brand new Webster at school everybody was one word and the definition said, "every person." Bill had rubbed his nose.

"Mr. Webster's dead. He can't help it if people messed up his dictionary. The words say every body."

To Bill that meant squirrels and rabbits and cats and birds and dogs—and pigs.

Daddy asked very quietly, "Did names sneak into your head for the rest of them too?"

Bill shoved his hands in his pockets. "Yessir. But Otis is the only one that adopted me."

"Oh, no," I whispered, really scared for Bill.

"I see," Daddy said. "He's adopted you."

It got so quiet that the katydids seemed to make a monstrous noise, and when our dog Brownie came bounding up the steps I almost jumped out of my skin.

"What you have done," Daddy said to Bill, "is to make that pig yours. From now on you are responsible for him."

"Will we have to. . . . When cold weather comes, will we . . .?"

Bill couldn't say it.

"Decisions are part of responsibility," Daddy said. "Let's sing 'New River Train.'"

I could not believe it, that Bill had gotten off that easily, and neither could Bill. When it came his turn to lead with, "Oh, darling, you can't love three," he sang so loud that the katydids shut up.

School didn't start until October so that the older kids would have a month to pick cotton. By that time Bill wished Daddy had punished him and not given him responsibility for Otis. Although they had been weaned for two months and were half as big as their mother, the other pigs stayed close to Mrs. Gruntling. Not Otis.

Bill filled in the hole Otis rooted under the fence. When that didn't work, he wired a board to the bottom of the fence. But Otis just found another place to root his way out.

Otis climbed into our tub of sun-warming bath water. Bill had to empty it and pump it full again. Correy and I were mad at Bill and Otis because we had to bathe in icy water.

Then Otis got a boil on his side. At first it was small, but day by day it grew bigger.

"I think you'd better ask Daddy what to do," Mother told Bill.

"Daddy knows about it," Bill said, blinking because he was determined not to cry.

Mother put her fingers under his chin and tilted his head so he would have to look at her. "It's your pig. It's up to you to ask for his help."

Bill jerked his chin away from her fingers. "I won't. I'll doctor him myself."

"I'll help," I said. "I'll put on a hot compress if you'll hold him."

"I don't think I can by myself," he said. "I'll go get LeRoy."

LeRoy lived only a quarter of a mile down the road, so Bill wasn't gone long. Instead of LeRoy, though, his sister Viola came. "LeRoy's helping Mama and Daddy pick cotton," she informed me, "so I come. I didn't want to, though. I don't want to hold no dirty old pig."

Neither Bill nor I said anything because we didn't want her to get peeved and go back home, but Otis was *not* dirty. He had shiny cherry-red bristles, and he liked to stay clean as much as Viola did.

I heated water and put salts in it the way Mother did when one of us had a boil. Mother gave me a cloth to make a compress and brought the pan of hot water outside. She was afraid we might spill the water and burn ourselves.

"You hold his front legs and I'll hold the hind ones," Bill told Viola.

Otis thought they were playing a game, but he wiggled because he didn't like to be still.

"Hurry, Meg," Bill said.

I dipped the compress into the hot water, squeezed it between my fingers to remove the excess water, and carefully laid it on the boil. It barely touched Otis. He gathered every muscle in his body, squealed right in Viola's ear, and bolted. It happened so quickly that I was still on my knees, holding the compress on empty air.

"He a strong little devil," Viola said. We were watching Otis run toward the cornfield, squealing at the top of his voice.

That night when Daddy came home, Bill asked for his help.

"All right," Daddy said. "We'll need a small sharp knife."

The first time Bill tried to speak, he only croaked. He cleared his throat and started over. "If we put a hot compress on it, maybe it'll open by itself."

"His hide is tough," Daddy said. "It won't open by itself."

Daddy got everything ready. "Meg, you can bring the antiseptic," he said.

"I didn't name him," I wanted to yell, but Daddy looked so grim I didn't open my mouth.

Daddy drove stakes into the ground and tied Otis's front and back legs to them. "The boil is making him miserable," he told Bill. "It has to be done." He didn't sound angry anymore, but gentle.

Otis was jerking his muscles and oinking, twisting his head from one side to the other. "Try to calm him, Son," Daddy said. "Wrap one arm around his neck and the other around his middle."

Bill positioned himself and kept murmuring to Otis that it would be all right, that it would soon be over.

Daddy struck a match and held the flame to the knife point.

"Ready?" Bill nodded.

Daddy made one quick jab into the side of the boil. Otis screamed so loud, I put my hands over my ears. Bill's face turned white, but he tightened his hold because Otis was trying so hard to break loose. Otis kept screaming while Daddy washed off the bloody pus and rubbed on antiseptic.

Otis sulked in the corner of the barn that night, but the next day he rooted out of the lot again. Bill gave up then on trying to keep Otis in the lot and let him chum around with Brownie.

Otis and Brownie were sleeping under the house on the Saturday afternoon when the rolling store came by.

Ordinarily, only two cars and a pickup truck ever came down the Blue Road, the road we lived on. It was named the Blue Road because when it rained the gumbo mud took on a bluish tinge. Nobody could drive on it when it rained because they would get stuck. The doctor and the plantation owner and the overseer drove on our road when it was dry, though.

Bill and I, Viola, and, supposedly, LeRoy, were playing kick-the-can in the front yard. LeRoy wouldn't stop blowing his harmonica long enough to chase, not even when we yelled at him. LeRoy was the oldest, twelve, so we couldn't make him do anything he didn't want to do.

We saw it way up the road. It looked like a huge river boat that had made a wrong turn onto dry land.

"What in the world?" Viola said and ran up on the porch. Viola's mother braided her hair in tiny pigtails all over her head. They were standing straight out, like there was a goosebump under each one.

"It's nothing to be frightened of," I told her. "Just some kind of truck."

She made a face at me. "Know-it-all Meg," she said.

Just before the contraption reached our house, the driver blew the horn at some chickens in the road. Brownie and Otis woke up and came out from under the house. The truck thundered by, rocking and weaving in the deep ruts. I didn't get a chance to read the writing on the side because of what happened. Brownie, with Otis right behind him, chased it! Brownie had never chased a car before.

Mother had come out on the porch.

"What was it, Miss Vera?" Viola asked.

"A rolling store," Mother said.

"Why didn't he stop?" I asked. "We might have wanted to buy something."

Mother laughed. "I expect he stopped earlier and discovered that the only money people on this road have is doodlum money—which is only good at the plantation store. Poor man. He wasted his time." Then she frowned. "I wonder what possessed Brownie to chase him."

A pig named Otis, I thought. I would have bet anything that it had been his notion.

Bill spanked Otis and Brownie. "Don't you ever do that again! You hear me?" he scolded.

Brownie drooped his head and tail, he

was so ashamed. I couldn't tell, but Bill said Otis was ashamed too.

Four days later, though, we realized that they had evidently thought the scolding was for not catching the rolling store. We had just gotten home from school when the plantation owner, Mr. Limon, drove by. Otis and Brownie tried harder that time and bit at his tires. Mr. Limon's eyes bugged out and he almost ran into the ditch. Mother said he had probably never been chased by a pig before.

Bill didn't try anymore to teach Brownie and Otis not to chase cars. Mother made some suggestions (I thought the best was to tie ropes around their necks and yank when they tried to), but Bill said never mind, that soon the road would be muddy. Then even the doctor would have to ride a mule to make his Blue Road calls.

It didn't rain all through October and into November, though, which was good because the cotton could be picked before the weather turned cold. Mother didn't go to the field to pick cotton, but Viola's mother, Aunt Louise, did. Viola's school was on the Blue Road, a mile nearer our homes than Bill's and my school. Her school let out at the same time ours did, but since her mother wouldn't know she hadn't come straight home, she often stayed until Bill or I came by so she could walk with us.

One day she played inside the school until she saw us through the window. Walking home, I cupped my hand over my nose because it was turning cold.

"Hog killing time," Viola said, looking at Bill, "for them that has a hog."

When she turned in to her house, I wouldn't say good-bye to her. Sometimes Viola could be mean.

When Bill and I got home, we knew the minute we saw her that Mother had a migraine headache. Her face was pale and pinched, and she kept pushing back her hair as if it hurt her head. She hadn't had one of the headaches for six months, and I had hoped they were gone forever.

"You'd better go lie down, Mother," I said. "I'll fix supper."

"Never mind the supper, Meg. Thank you. Aunt Louise is home. You-all go play with Viola and LeRoy awhile." Her fingers trembled as she began to unbutton her dress. "And take the pig with you, please. He's been trying to get inside all day."

She didn't mention taking Brownie, but he went everywhere Bill did except to school.

While Bill and I were changing our clothes, Correy whined, and on the way to Aunt Louise's he wanted me to carry him. I wouldn't, so I had to practically drag him. Bill didn't help a bit. He played with Brownie and Otis. Especially Otis. They chased each other in a circle, then Bill told him to count to three by tapping his foot. When he did it right Bill patted him and bragged, "He's really smart."

"Oh, sure," I said, "it takes real brains to count to three."

About an hour after we arrived at Aunt Louise's, Uncle Samuel came in.

"Your daddy's home too," he told us. "Last of the cotton's on the way to gin— for which I thanks the Lord. Old Jack Frost's goin' breathe hard on us tonight." He rubbed his burr-pricked fingers. "Ain't nothing more painful than picking cotton on a cold morning."

A little later Daddy brought quilts and a paper bag with our nightclothes and toothbrushes in it. The last time Mother had had a migraine headache, we'd stayed at Aunt Louise's for two days and nights. Daddy had gone to the store that time and called Dr. Spain.

I was thinking about that while Daddy talked to Aunt Louise about Mother, "... that a falling feather sounds like a crashing oak tree. You're sure you don't mind, Louise?"

"A' course we don't mind," Aunt Louise told him. "We happy to have them."

Well, I'm not happy to stay, I thought. I want to go home. I want to sleep in my own bed.

Viola tried to be cheerful all the way through supper—squirrel and rice stew— but I wouldn't talk. About the only thing I said was that I was glad tomorrow was Saturday. Bill said he liked the stew a lot, and after supper he thanked Aunt Louise. Bill, I thought, always did the right thing. I couldn't stand him.

"Well, I think I'll walk up to the boardin' house," said Uncle Samuel. "Listen to some piano playing."

"Just see you don't drink none a' that lightning they got at the boarding house," Aunt Louise told him, and he laughed and kissed her cheek.

After he had gone, Aunt Louise lit the lamps and said she would make the pallets down directly.

I heard Otis coming up the back steps and said, "It's probably that pig's fault Mother got a migraine headache."

"Yeah," Viola said. "Listen to him. Askin' to come into the kitchen."

"He's cold," Bill said.

"He ain't that cold, Bill," Aunt Louise said. She opened the door and pushed Otis with the broom. "Go on, pig. Go under the house with Brownie." You could tell by the way he grunted that he didn't want to do that, but he went back down the steps.

"Was he my pig, I'd whup him," Viola told Bill.

"Be careful you don't hurt Bill's feelings by not calling him Otis," I said sarcastically. "Him and his 'every body should have a name.'"

Bill and LeRoy were building a matchstick house on the floor, but LeRoy stopped and took his harmonica out of his pocket.

"This number be dedicated to Bill," he announced, and began playing, slowly and mournfully, "Nobody knows the trouble I've seen, nobody knows my sorrow ..."

Aunt Louise, rocking Correy like he was a baby, looked from one of us to the other. "Why you young'uns pickin' on Bill? It just so happens me and him got the same notions. All God's creatures is special. I always return to earth some proud part of a animal. Them squirrels we ate tonight, their tails is buried in the back yard. And there's rooster combs and rabbit ears."

"That's nice," Bill said. I bit my lip. In my rotten mood I had almost said that with Otis she would have a choice—his tail or his snout.

I went to bed with confused anger still bubbling inside me. Mother shouldn't have gotten sick. Bill shouldn't have let Otis adopt him. It couldn't turn cold—it wasn't fair.

We slept late the next morning, until eight o'clock. Uncle Samuel was still asleep, but Aunt Louise said not to worry about being quiet, that a freight train running through the house wouldn't wake him on a morning he didn't have to go to work.

While Aunt Louise fixed breakfast, Bill and LeRoy folded the pallet quilts in the front room, and I helped Viola make the beds in her and LeRoy's room. I had slept in LeRoy's bed; he had slept on a pallet. Viola and I worked without talking, and every now and then I glanced toward the window. Winter had come. You could see the frost covering the fields.

After Viola went to the front room where Aunt Louise had a warm fire going, I closed my eyes and leaned my forehead against the cold window glass. Poor Bill. It seemed like such a short time ago when he had told Daddy about naming Otis. I could see Bill's bare feet, his toes curling under when he tried to ask what would happen when it turned cold. But Daddy had said, "Decisions are part of responsibility." He must have meant that Bill could be the one to decide. Probably he could keep Otis for a pet until he died of old age!

Feeling better, I lifted my head, rubbed away the fog my breath had made on the pane, and saw a car turning off of the main road onto the Blue Road. A car was coming! Without waiting to identify it, I whirled around and ran.

"Bill, a car . . ."

He charged out the door before I finished, with LeRoy and Viola and I right behind him. Bill scooted under the house and held Brownie. When Otis tried to get to the road, LeRoy ran back and forth in front of him, waving his arms.

It was Dr. Spain, looking straight ahead, driving fast the way he always did. He stopped in front of our house.

"Come on, children," Aunt Louise called from the front door. "Flapjacks is ready."

Bill came to where I was standing by the side of the road. We watched Dr. Spain get out of his car and go into our house.

Since we had come out without our jackets, we were shivering. Bill touched my arm. "Come on, Meg."

Inside, Bill picked up his jacket. "Maybe I'd better wait outside until the doctor leaves," he said to Aunt Louise.

"He most likely won't come back this way," she said. "Drive on and take Ridge Road back to the highway; make some other stops along the way."

Aunt Louise guessed wrong. We were almost through eating when all of us froze, our ears catching the sounds: Brownie and Otis moving fast from under the house, a car going past, a stomach-sinking thud.

"Coats," Aunt Louise shouted. She scooped up Correy and we all went out. A hundred feet past the house Dr. Spain had stopped the car. Otis was lying beside the road.

I ran the other way—home. When I went in, Daddy put a finger to his lips. "She's sleeping," he whispered with a smile in his eyes. "When she wakes up, she'll be fine."

A heaviness I hadn't realized was there drained out of me. Then I remembered why I had come and told Daddy what had happened.

Before we got there, we saw Dr. Spain down on one knee, his stethoscope on Otis's chest. He straightened up as we arrived.

"Sorry, Harth," he said to Daddy, "but at least it was a clean blow. Fatal concussion, edible except for the brain."

Daddy sighed. "It was bound to happen."

Bill's face, all twisted out of kilter, made it plain that Otis had belonged to him. And, although he didn't say anything, he might as well have been accusing the doctor of murder.

"Look, boy," Dr. Spain said gruffly, "I don't like suffering. That's why I'm a doctor. Be glad he went fast."

The angry part of Bill's expression dissolved and he wiped his arm across his eyes. He knew it was not the doctor's fault.

Dr. Spain left. The rest of us just stood there, first on one foot, then on the other, shivering. Finally, Bill spoke to Daddy.

"You said what to do with Otis was my decision. Could we bury him, like we would if it was Brownie?"

For a minute Daddy didn't answer. I thought he was going to say, "As poor as people are, as hard as we all work for food . . ." Things like that. But he didn't.

"Yes," he said.

"Is it too late to sell him?"

"No," Daddy answered, "I can dress him out, then borrow the pickup to take the pork to the market in town."

Bill looked down at his feet. "I don't want to do either one. I want to give him to Aunt Louise."

Aunt Louise started to protest, but Daddy nodded to show that Bill's decision pleased him. Aunt Louise put her hand on Bill's shoulder to thank him. It would be Otis's tail she would bury, I thought. His proud, curly tail.

Bill buttoned his jacket and he and Brownie started away. He stopped and turned around like he wanted to say something else, but he couldn't trust his voice.

"It's all right," Daddy said gently. "Go on to the woods. Just don't stay too long and get chilled."

But Bill kept standing there, and finally he squeezed out, "I wouldn't have kept him anyway."

When Bill came home his eyes were red and his face splotched. We hugged each other. I had cried about Otis too. So had Mother and Correy.

It was good to settle into my own bed that night. From his bed, Correy's deep-sleep breathing came within minutes. But I could hear the springs creaking from Bill's bed and knew he was restless.

"Meg?"

"Uh-hum."

"I've made up my mind about something."

At last, I thought, Bill had learned about not naming.

"When another litter comes," he said, "I'm going to name one of them Otis Gruntling the Second."

I was about to protest, but the springs had stopped creaking—Bill had fallen asleep.

The Valentine

My first thought when the new boy came into the classroom was that we girls had wasted a lot of time fussing with our hair. My second thought was that Miss Gibson hadn't been fair to us; she should have described him when she told us he would be coming.

"Class," Miss Gibson said, "this is Talmadge McLinn. His family has just moved here from eastern Tennessee." Neither her voice nor her expression threatened us, but her eyes, sweeping from one side of the room to the other, made it clear that we had better mind our manners.

"From Wild Hog Holler, to be exact," Talmadge said.

Maxine giggled and others sniggered. Miss Gibson glared at us and the sniggering faded out. I figured Maxine, who giggled about everything, was probably choking herself.

Talmadge's feet were so big, they called even more attention to his clubbed right foot. Clubfeet were not unusual, but I had never seen one like his. His weight came down on the outside of his little toe so that his heel was raised up about two inches from the floor even when he was standing still. He was wearing hightop work shoes—without socks, despite the January cold. His shabby overalls stopped before they reached the tops of his shoes. The other boys wore their best clothes, generally corduroy pants and blue shirts, to school.

Talmadge's hair, which reminded me of winter-dried grass, was longer than any I

had ever seen on a boy. It hung down the
back of his neck and hid the tops of his
ears. His smile stretched from one side of
his face to the other, offering all of us his
friendship, asking for ours. I knew how he
felt because I remembered how the kids
had looked at me the first day I had come
to this school. They had made such fun of
my citified clothes—especially my neat
new oxfords—that I had gone home and
beat them with Daddy's taphammer to
make them look old. Like Talmadge, I had
seemed foreign to the other kids. I glanced
straight into his eyes, which were very
blue, to let him know I sympathized with
him.

"Which cheer ye want I should set in?"
Talmadge asked Miss Gibson, and Stinky
Sterret burst out laughing. Miss Gibson
sent him out into the hall.

Stinky, I thought, had forgotten that
when he had first come from Oklahoma
the other boys had ragged him until he'd

turned mean and earned the name Stinky.

At recess we girls talked about Talmadge. "I feel sorry for him," Josie said.

Maxine went into a fit of giggles. "But do you want him for a boyfriend?"

Josie tossed 'her head. "I have more boyfriends now than I know what to do with. I just said I feel sorry for him."

"Me too," I said. Since Josie and I were best friends, we practically always agreed with each other. "I don't think any of the boys will make friends with him — and Stinky is going to make his life miserable."

Stinky did too, beginning that very recess. He ran by Talmadge, grabbed his cap, and threw it to Raymond. Talmadge seemed to think it was a game and kept grinning and trying to recapture his cap while other boys joined in to keep it away from him. Some of the boys held the cap out to him and waited until Talmadge awkwardly reached them and held out his hand before tossing it to someone else. C.C. got a big laugh when he examined the inside of the cap, widened his eyes, and threw it quickly, shaking his fingers like the cap had lice in it.

We girls didn't think it was very funny, except for Maxine. We kept watching, though, waiting to see what would happen.

The smile on Talmadge's face held even when Stinky caught the cap, pinched it on his nose, and blew. That's when Miss Gibson, who had been standing close to the door talking to another teacher, stepped in. Walking fast, her head thrust forward like a snapping turtle's, she charged into the middle of the group, snatched the cap away from Stinky, and shoved him backward so hard he fell.

Maxine put her fist in her mouth.

You shouldn't have done that, Miss Gibson, I thought. From now on Stinky will make Talmadge his enemy.

Talmadge knew that too. Wiping his cap on the dead grass, he said, "Hit don't make no never mind." He settled the cap back on his head. "There now. Hit's good as new. They was just funnin', Miss Gibson."

Stinky might have been funning before. But now his mouth turned down at the corners in hate.

In class Talmadge grew quieter and quieter during the next two weeks. His hand stopped shooting up to answer questions; he stayed in during recess and read rather than go outside.

John Edward, the boy I liked best, didn't act mean to Talmadge. He didn't seem to mind that Talmadge made a hundred in almost every test except arithmetic, either. It didn't surprise me. John Edward had never held it against me when I sat him down in spelling bees. One or the other of us had always been the last to go down until Talmadge came along. I couldn't understand how somebody who couldn't talk right could spell so well. Talmadge spelled both of us down two times out of every three.

While John Edward wasn't mean to Tal-

madge and talked to him, he didn't make
friends with him. Nobody did. I stayed
away from him too until Mother sent a
note one day that I had had an earache
the night before and couldn't go outside to
play. At first Miss Gibson was in the room
with Talmadge and me; then she left to go
to the library. Her feet were still tapping
down the hall when Talmadge, carrying
the book he was reading, came up to a
desk in the next row from mine and
sidled into it.

"I'm sorry ye're feeling porely, Meg,"
he said.

"Oh, I'm all right," I said. "I had an
earache last night. It's gone except for a
twinge now and then."

"My sister gits earaches too," he said.
"They must be awful." He looked so con-
cerned he made me fidget.

"Ye ever read this here book?" he asked
me.

I glanced at the door and listened hard
to see if any of the kids were hanging

around in the hall. The only sounds were the muted squeals and laughter from the school grounds.

"I don't think so," I said, and turned my head to the side to read the title. *Bob, Son of Battle,* it said. There was a picture of a collie dog's face under the title. "Is it about a dog that fights a lot?"

Talmadge chuckled as if the question pleased him. "That there word Battle throws ye, don't it? Hit did me too. Battle was the name of the dog's daddy. A gray dog—sheep dog—he was."

"Oh," I said.

Talmadge turned from his place at about the middle of the book to the front pages and handed the book over to me.

"See, that's whar ye start cotching on— where they compare Bob with Rex, Son of Rally."

I silently read the paragraph he pointed to:

> "Ay, the Gray Dogs, bless 'em!"
> the old man was saying. "Yo canna

beat 'em not nohow. Known 'em
ony time this sixty year, I have, and
niver knew a bad un yet. Not as I
say, mind ye, as any on 'em cooms
up to Rex son o' Rally. Ah, he was
a one, was Rex! We's never won Cup
since his day."

I handed the book to Talmadge. "It's
hard to read."

"At first it is," he said, "but ye'd soon
git the hang of it. I ain't never lent it out
before, but ye kin borry it when I'm done
this time." He turned some pages and read
aloud,

"Did yo' feyther beat yo' last night?"
she inquired in a low voice, and
there was a shade of anxiety in the
soft brown eyes.

"Nay," the boy answered; "he was a
goin' to, but he niver did. Drunk,"
he added in explanation.

It sounded like music when Talmadge
read it. "You talk kind of like them," I
said.

He nodded. "The Thorntons—my mother

was a Thornton—come from the Dalelands like them." He turned sideways in the desk and leaned toward me, his hands folded between his knees. "Dalesmen air from England," he explained. "My dad's people was from across the border—in Scotland. Fer back the Thorntons and the McLinns spilt blood feudin' one with t'other. So when my mother and father got married, neither side would have aught to do with them. Mother used to cry a lot about it. The feudin' ain't never quit, albeit my father says cain't any two people tell the same tale about why it commenced in the first place."

"Oh," I said. I didn't know what else to say. It seemed so important to him that I added, "They were mean to treat your mother and father that way."

Talmadge sat up straight again and stroked the book with his fingertips. "I got this here book fer Christmas when I was but a tyke. I'm just now gittin' to the point

I can read it good." After a pause, he said, "I'm glad my father don't beat me like David's does in the book. My dad's not a drunk neither."

I knew why he told me that. As if it were some awful scandal, Maxine had informed us that his father made corn whiskey out on the uncleared land where Talmadge's family lived. I wondered if he helped his father make moonshine, but it wouldn't be polite to ask. Besides, there was something I wanted to know more.

"Talmadge—aren't you going to fight him?"

He didn't pretend he didn't know whom I was talking about. A week ago, in front of the whole class, Stinky had challenged Talmadge to come behind the ditchbank and fight. Since then Stinky and the three boys who hung around with him had made remarks about Talmadge being yellow.

Talmadge closed the book and shook his head. "We come here to git away from fightin' much as to make a livin'. I seen enough fightin' to last me a lifetime. We'uns just want to live peaceable." He traced his finger around the picture of the dog's face on the front of the book. "I've took a vow not to never fight agin." Glancing at me, he said, "I ain't told nobody else except John Edward."

"I won't tell," I said. "John Edward won't either."

The bell rang; I grabbed my science book and pretended to be studying. Talmadge started back toward his desk. Too late. Maxine was standing in the doorway, her bird eyes darting from one of us to the other. She and her best friend Bonnie Lou walked by my desk and, as if she were speaking privately to Maxine, but loud enough for others coming in to hear, Bonnie Lou said, "Look's like Meg has a new sweetheart." Maxine bent over from the waist, she giggled so hard.

For the rest of the day they and some of

the other girls wrote notes to each other about Talmadge and me. I managed to ignore them, which I knew worked best, but sometimes it was hard. I kept wishing John Edward would give me the new whistling ring he had brought to school and shown around that morning. Everybody knew Bonnie Lou spent half her time writing his name in her notebook.

When the last bell rang I quickly gathered my books. Most of the time when the weather was nice I went the long way home, around by the post office and the store, so I could be with Josie. Today, though, I intended to walk the short, direct way home with Grace Bowers. Grace lived on the other side of me on the Blue Road. She never tarried on the schoolground, so I had to hurry. I was about to put my coat on when Miss Gibson said, "Meg."

"Yes, ma'am."

"How do you feel?"

"Fine," I said.

"Good. You evidently forgot that this is your day to empty the wastebasket."

I worked my way through the crowded hall, emptied the wastebasket into the big trash can, and ran back. Ignoring the people still in the room, I put on my coat and scarf and pulled my cap down over my ears.

Talmadge, wearing an overcoat that came almost to his ankles and made him look like a scarecrow dressed for winter, came over to me.

"Ye look right dauncy, Meggie," he said.

I could feel my cheeks turn pink. Several boys, including Stinky, were in a huddle at the back of the room, and I had an uneasy feeling that it had something to do with Talmadge. The last thing I wanted was for them to think there was any truth in what Bonnie Lou and Maxine had been saying about my liking Talmadge.

"I've got to hurry," I said, and scooted out the door.

Before I had reached the road, much less caught up with Grace, I sensed excitement behind me, turned to look, and found myself going back. I didn't like fistfights— my stomach had already tightened up— but something seemed to pull me to watch.

I saw immediately what had happened. Stinky had come up behind Talmadge and yanked his *Bob, Son of Battle* book out of his hand. For the first time since he had started to our school, all of the meakness went out of Talmadge.

"Give it back," he said, his voice so commanding that it took Stinky by surprise.

Talmadge was taller than Stinky, but he had the bad foot. In addition, Stinky could make his biceps muscle jump when he bent his arm at the elbow and knotted his fist. He showed off that way a lot. Most of the boys were afraid of him. When he had finally turned on them for tormenting him about being an Okie, he had won three fights in one afternoon. I didn't figure Talmadge had much of a chance.

Talmadge held out his hand for the book. For a minute Stinky looked like he was going to give it back to him, but the other boys were nudging him, saying things like, "Git him, Stinky!" "Go on." "Make him show his yellow streak."

John Edward didn't do that, but he didn't make a move to stop it like he had other times either. He licked his lips, glancing from Stinky to Talmadge.

Stinky dropped the book and kicked it to the side. "You want it, hillbilly, pick it up!" he said.

A tremor passed through Talmadge, but because of our conversation at morning recess I realized that it didn't come from fear. It came from fighting within himself. It struck me that John Edward knew that too.

In one move, like a mother wildcat I had seen spring at a dog who had come too close to her cubs, Talmadge shucked his coat, took a step forward, and hit Stinky high on the jaw. Stinky staggered and the people watching gasped with surprise. Stinky recovered quickly, though, lowered his head, and charged, swinging hard. Talmadge moved in a circle, ducking and swaying to dodge Stinky's fists. Even when Stinky's blows landed, they were short or glancing. Talmadge didn't move his head back enough once, though, and his nose began to dribble blood.

Kids from other classes were there now too, some silent, some shouting to stop it, others egging them on. The smell of nervous sweat from all the bodies made me feel like I was going to throw up. But I stayed, even shoved people aside who tried to get in front of me.

Talmadge had only thrown one punch, but suddenly his fist shot out again. He hit Stinky in the same place on his jaw. Stinky went down. Talmadge took a couple of long awkward steps and straddled him, pinning his shoulders to the ground. He had won!

And then Talmadge did a terrible thing.

He started to cry. Holding his arm over his eyes and his bleeding nose, he got up off of Stinky, picked up his book, and walked away.

Some of the crowd, led by Stinky's friends, were shouting, "Go back to Wild Hog Holler!" I took a few steps toward Talmadge. You did the right thing, I wanted to tell him. You had to stand up for yourself.

The kids were all staring at me. "Go back to Wild Hog Holler!" I yelled just once before I ran—toward the Blue Road and home.

Generally a fight was the topic of conversation the next day, but nobody mentioned the one between Talmadge and Stinky. It was like we all wanted to forget what had happened. I kept thinking about John Edward, who was known as a peacemaker, and the way he had licked his lips when Talmadge and Stinky were about to fight. I finally worked it out. He hadn't been excited about the possibility of their fighting, but about whether or not Talmadge could stick to his vow. I decided I liked another boy, Tom Garrity, better than I did John Edward.

I didn't want to talk with Talmadge after that day, though. He was too different; he didn't belong. John Edward looked through him. Nobody included him, or bothered him. He had become an outcast. When I knew he was looking at me, I pretended to be busy with my school work. When he walked beside me as we were leaving the building, I answered him politely and hurried away as soon as I could.

"It's just politeness, that's all it is," I explained to Grace as we were walking home in a cold drizzling rain. "Mother and Daddy have drummed being polite and kind into me since I was born, so I can't help it."

Grace didn't answer. This was one of her silent days. I jabbered about other things, about Miss Gibson and Josie's new haircut and Bonnie Lou's spitefulness. We had walked another quarter of a mile before Grace said, "Meg, you ain't being honest. You really like Talmadge."

"I don't like him! I can't stand him!"

Grace shrugged and said nothing more.

Finally I broke the silence. "You know good and well that if I showed that I liked him, the other kids would peck me raw."

Grace still didn't say anything, just looked at me with sad, old eyes.

I couldn't be mean to Grace, though, even when she treated me like I was a silly little kid. She had befriended me before anybody else at school had accepted me. And I knew about her life at home. She had to tend the babies and scrub floors and wash clothes when she wasn't chopping and picking cotton. I had seen the bruises on her back from her father's razor strop. So at my house, I just said, "See you tomorrow."

She nodded and walked on, her head bent against the icy drizzle. I knew I didn't have to worry about Grace telling anyone that I had admitted I liked Talmadge. I didn't tell her secrets to other people, not even to Josie, and she didn't tell mine.

With Valentine's Day coming up, I began to get especially nervous about Talmadge. If he brought me a mushy valentine I would just die.

Miss Gibson tried to skip having a valentine box altogether, but we argued so well she gave in. "It's the only fun thing we have between Christmas and the end-of-school plays," Maxine said. "After all," Josie added, "this is the last year. From seventh grade up we can't have a valentine box." "It's a tradition," Peggy explained in her sighing, tired voice.

Miss Gibson picked Peggy, a girl everybody liked okay but didn't choose as best friend, to make the valentine box.

Mother had never liked valentine boxes, not even for first grade, much less sixth. Considering that, I should have known better than to fuss about having to make my own valentines.

"All the kids who live up on the highway get theirs in town," I told her.

"With money so scarce, that must be a sacrifice," she said.

I grumbled under my breath and she turned on me. "You can either make them from the wallpaper book or forget it. And if you make one, you have to make them for every person in the class."

The next morning I hesitated before approaching the box, considering holding out Stinky's and Bonnie Lou's and Maxine's and Talmadge's. Peggy had made a pretty last box. She had wrapped it in white crepe paper and pasted red composition-paper hearts of different sizes all over it. Oh, what the heck, I decided. I might as well end it by giving a valentine to everybody. I dropped all my envelopes through the slot.

Miss Gibson didn't hand out the valentines until the last period, and by that time I was a wreck. I had started imagining that I would only get four or five, believing that nobody really liked me. I got thirteen. Peggy and Josie and John Edward got more, but I didn't feel too bad. The one from Tom Garrity was store-bought with an elephant on the front. "I've got a trunkful of love for you, Valentine," it said. And between the valentine and the inside of the envelope nestled a stick of Doublemint chewing gum. I couldn't wait to show Bonnie Lou and Maxine. Neither of them had given me a valentine.

I felt sorry for Talmadge and was glad I had made a valentine for him. Mine had been one of the three he received. I had just printed "Happy Valentine's Day" in red and signed my name. There was no way the kids could make something of that, I thought.

Talmadge did though. He caught up with me on the front steps as we were leaving school.

"Shore makes a feller feel good to git a valentine from a blossom-eyed gal like you, Meg," he said. "I hope hit don't fret ye that I didn't give you one. I didn't give nary one—couldn't git around to making any."

"That's all right," I said quickly and, turning my back to him, started talking to Peggy.

At home I dropped my valentines in my top dresser drawer for keepsakes. I had put them and Valentine's Day and the valentine box out of my mind by the next day.

When we woke up Saturday morning, Daddy said, "I think it's going to snow." Bill and Correy and I prayed that it would, and after it finally started in mid-afternoon, we prayed that it would stick. It kept melting as fast as it hit the ground, though, and I got too cold to play outside anymore. Besides, the ground had gotten sticky wet.

Mother said I could help her quilt if I worked slowly and carefully. I pulled a stool up to the quilting frame. Outside the wind moaned softly around the corners of the house, but in the front room where we were quilting the heater glowed pink on its sides. The house smelled of burning wood and the gingerbread Mother had baked.

Cozy and happy, I didn't even look up when Brownie gave a warning growl from the front porch. Daddy came up behind me and ducked down to peer past my shoulder out the window. At that moment I heard a call: "Hello!" My head jerked up. There, beside the road, stood Talmadge. He was wearing the ugly long coat and his cap—and somebody had cut his hair. It looked awful, like it had been chopped off with his cap as a guideline.

I slid off the stool, and one of those miserable burning blushes I couldn't do a thing about raced from my neck right up to my hairline.

"It's the new boy in our class," I said. "Talmadge."

Daddy went to the door, his face crinkling with amusement at my embarrassment, which made it worse.

"Come on in," Daddy called as warmly as if Talmadge were Mr. Limon, the plantation owner.

Talmadge came over the footbridge, scraped the blue-tinged mud off his shoes on the front steps, took his cap off and stuffed it in his right pocket, and came inside, nodding and smiling. His nose was red and his eyes were teared from the cold.

"This is Talmadge," I said stiffly. "He moved here from Tennessee."

"From Wild Hog Holler, to be exact," Talmadge said, smiling all over his face.

Mother smiled back at him. Daddy chuckled with a merriment that matched Talmadge's.

"I know your father," Daddy said. "Fine man. Go on over by the heater and get warm, Talmadge."

Talmadge held his hands to the heater a minute, then turned his back to it. His nose had started to drip. He wiggled his hand into his overcoat pocket, took out a white rag, and blew his nose.

"Take Talmadge's coat for him, Meg," Mother said. There was a puzzled note in her voice, as if she didn't understand why I seemed to have forgotten the art of making welcome.

"I believe I'll keep it on awhile," Talmadge said. "I'm chilled clear to the marrow."

Bill and Correy came bursting in through the kitchen from the back yard, puffing and laughing.

"Talmadge!" Bill exclaimed, "What're you doing here?"

"Hi, Bill," Talmadge said.

It didn't surprise me that Bill knew Talmadge—kids in the lower grades often knew the ones above them. It did surprise me that Talmadge knew Bill.

Correy was staring at Talmadge's clubfoot. Mother should teach him not to do that, I thought. It isn't polite.

"That's Correy," Bill and I said at the same time, his tone proud and cheerful, mine forced. Talmadge squatted down, one knee up, one down, man fashion, so he would be eye-level with Correy.

"Hi, Correy." He pointed at his foot. "Hit were like that when I come into this world." Standing up, he winked at Correy. "Don't slow me down none, though."

Then he walked straight over to me, to the spot where I stood like an upright board, reached into his left overcoat pocket, took out a big white envelope, and handed it to me.

"I hitched into town this morning and bought this," he said.

Fumbling, I opened the envelope.

"Hit's a valentine," Talmadge said. "Since Valentine's Day has done passed, I got it for half price. With money I saved up myself."

The valentine was beautiful, lacy with delicate flowers and hearts on the front. Inside it said, "To My Sweetheart."

"I was goin' to git one that said 'To My Friend,'" Talmadge said nervously, "but they didn't have none like that."

With his bad foot he had walked miles in bitter weather to bring a valentine to me. It made my throat ache. As I continued to gaze silently at the valentine, I could tell that he was waiting for me to say something. Mother and Daddy and Bill and Correy were waiting too, waiting for me to thank Talmadge and ask him to stay and have gingerbread and buttermilk with us.

I relaxed. If the kids at school found out about Talmadge bringing the valentine, I would laugh and say, "I thought I would die!"

"It's the prettiest valentine I ever saw," I said. "Thank you very much."

Talmadge's naked ears turned red. He put his hands in his pockets and rocked back and forth, beaming like he heard a song playing in his head.

Smiling, I asked, "Would you like to

have some gingerbread and buttermilk with us?"

"Shore is a temptation," Talmadge said, "but I've got to git on home. Been gone so long I 'spect my mother's as worrified as a tabbycat what's lost one a' her kits."

"At least take a piece with you," Mother said. She went quickly into the kitchen and came back with a big square of the cake.

We watched out the window as Talmadge started up the road eating gingerbread. The snow had almost fizzled out, and the sun was sparkling around the edges of broken clouds.

"I'm proud of you," Daddy said to me in a soft, pleased voice. "Proud that you choose your friends according to what's inside them. I've heard about the way the lad's been shunned."

I stared down at the floor, too ashamed to lift my head. I could see Talmadge sitting hunched at his desk, his eyes pleading with me to be his friend; I could hear myself shouting, "Go back to Wild Hog Holler!"

"It took courage not to go along with the crowd," Daddy said and reached out to touch me.

"Don't—please." My words came out sounding choked.

I hurried into my room and scrambled into my coat, then ran blindly outside to the barn and climbed up to the loft. The fragrant, loose hay gave under my weight, bouncing back up behind me as I crawled across it, cradling me when I sank down into it, muffling the sound when I said, "Talmadge, I'm sorry," and let the tears burst free.

Lady Merida

"Cross over," Josie said.

Her commanding tone aggravated me and I didn't see any reason to walk on the far side of the road just because Mrs. Merida was playing the piano. But which side of the road we walked on didn't seem like a big enough reason to fight with my best friend. I crossed over.

Mrs. Merida lived with Mr. Limon, the plantation owner, and her daughter, the lady from England he had married. Josie remembered the first Mrs. Limon, who had died before my family moved to Arkansas. "It depressed him so bad," Josie had told me, "that he went across the ocean for a vacation—and came back with a new wife."

People didn't say anything in front of Mr. Limon—times were too hard to chance getting put off the plantation—but his mother-in-law made a fine subject for talk behind his back. Some said Mrs. Merida was moonstruck, others came right out with crazy. And she had cancer. They said the cancer and the craziness went together.

Mrs. Merida never visited neighbors or went to the store or to the post office, but some of the kids had seen her walking in the Limons' flower garden. And everybody had heard her playing the piano, which they cited as proof of her madness. Not that we hadn't heard pianos—including the one at school, there were four on the plantation—but none of them sounded anything like Mrs. Merida's. Her music whispered and thundered, stroked and lashed, danced and wept. It made me dream, made me restless, made my heart

and my mind yearn for something beyond
their ken.

"She's really..." Josie traced a little
circle by her temple when we were past
the house.

Set in a grove of oak trees, the Limon
house was painted white and had a
screened front porch. There were shrubs
too, and roses climbing a trellis, and a
curving sandy walkway to the front steps.
I looked back over my shoulder at the
house, walking as slowly as I could so I
could hear the piano.

"Mother says she's just eccentric," I said.
Mother had never met Mrs. Merida, but
she knew Mrs. Limon and liked her.

Josie bounced her hair, which was thick
and wavy and the color of a red squirrel.
"Well, Papa says she's crazy—and I guess
he knows."

Josie's father, Mr. Tomkin, was a ginner,
an important position on the plantation.
She said that was why he knew all about
the lives of the other important people. I

liked Mr. Tomkin, but I didn't think it was very nice of him to talk about Mrs. Merida.

Josie put her face so close to mine I could count her freckles. "And furthermore, he says that terrible disease she has is contagious." She bounced her hair again. "That's why she never visits anybody, or even goes to the post office."

Josie's know-it-all attitude and her bossiness really bothered me. Lately it had gotten worse, as if she was trying to see how far she could push me. But I didn't like to argue and I didn't know what to say in Mrs. Merida's defense—for all I knew, maybe Mrs. Merida's disease *was* contagious—so I kept quiet.

After I got home I waited until Bill and Correy went outside to play. Then I told Mother what Mr. Tomkin had said about Mrs. Merida's illness being contagious. Mother was setting up the ironing board and she jerked the legs so hard I thought they would break.

"That's bosh and nonsense!" she exploded. "Cancer is not contagious!" Pulling one of my school dresses over the ironing board, she said, "Meg, would you sweep the kitchen. The clothes have been sprinkled so long they're going to mildew if I don't get them done."

"Sure," I said. I knew she would return to the subject. She only wanted to make the right sentences in her head.

Mother took a flatiron off the stove and touched it with a tongue-moistened finger. The moisture sizzled, she began to iron, and the kitchen filled with a clean, starchy smell.

"People don't mean to be cruel," she said. "It's just that Mrs. Merida and her music are different, so they don't understand them. What they don't understand, they fear; and what they fear, they disparage."

I didn't know the word disparage, but if I asked what it meant she would just tell me to look it up. I had a fair idea about the meaning from the way she had used it, though, so I nodded and reached the broom under the table to sweep out some cornbread crumbs.

"Actually," I told her, "I think Mrs. Merida's music is wonderful, even if you can't clap your hands or sing to it. I don't care what Josie says."

Mother worked the iron around the dress collar. "So do I. Sometimes late at night, when it's still, I can hear it through the bedroom window—so beautiful, so filled with passion." She gave a sad little sigh. "I think Mrs. Merida must play when she's in pain."

"I'd give anything if I could play the piano like that," I said.

"Then why don't you ask her to give you lessons?"

I stopped sweeping and stared at Mother. Even though I didn't believe most of them, considering the number of stories, Mrs. Merida must be at least a wee bit mad. Besides, she was a very important person, and she lived in a very important house. Just thinking about going there was scary ... and kind of exciting.

Mother set the cooled flatiron back on the stove and picked up the other one. "Meg, believe me—there's nothing to be alarmed about. In fact, the one way Josie's own mother defies her husband is to visit Mrs. Merida."

This time I figured Mother had gotten some wrong information. I couldn't imagine Josie's spiritless, dried-up little mother defying Mr. Tomkin. She could be in the middle of fixing supper and Mr. Tomkin would call from his easy chair in the living room, "Sarah, bring me a glass of water," and without a word she'd stop her work and take him the water. I thought of Mrs. Tomkin as a servant when I thought of her at all.

"Mrs. Tomkin and Mrs. Merida are friends," Mother was saying. "But you must not mention that to anybody—especially not to Josie. Mr. Tomkin pretends he doesn't know, and as long as he thinks no one else knows, it's all right."

I was going to ask her to repeat slowly what she had just said, but the boys charged through the back door, Correy chasing Bill, and ran right through my nice pile of dirt. I threw the broom after them, but I wasn't really all that angry. I knew now how to stand up to Josie! And I would learn to play the piano at the same time.

The next afternoon I left Josie standing on the other side of the road and went up the sandy walkway through the grove of oak trees to the Limon house. Josie had tried to talk me out of it and said she might walk with Peggy's group from now on if I went. That scared me, but it also made me more determined.

It was reassuring to find that the Limons' screened porch creaked just like the porch on our Blue Road house. Mrs. Limon answered my knock. Up close I could see why Mr. Limon had brought her from

England. She looked like a movie star, with creamy skin and cornflower-blue eyes and a nicely rounded bosom.

Clutching my books so tightly that my arm cramped, I stammered, "I—I'm Meg Weston. I wanted to—to talk to your mother about, uh, taking piano lessons."

"Why, yes," she said. "If Mama—that is, nothing like this has happened before."

"Dorothy," a voice behind her said, "will you get out of the doorway so the girl can come in." I liked their accents and wished I could talk that way.

"Hello, Mrs. Merida," I said.

"Lady Merida. Lady Rose Merida."

"Yes, Ma'am, Lady Merida."

She was wearing a soft and shimmery gray dress that went all the way to the floor, but it was only old fashioned, not crazy. She had not torn out hunks of her own hair, as I had heard, and there was no blood dripping from her fingertips either. Her nails were just painted with bright red polish.

Feeling more confident, I continued my inspection. I wanted to be able to describe Lady Merida to Mother. She was terribly thin. Her gray, tightly curled hair topped a small face, and her pale skin was drawn tight over her bones.

Then Lady Merida stepped toward me and my confidence dissolved. Her fierce gaze made the hairs on the back of my neck stand straight out.

"Well, I—I didn't think you would, I mean could, Ma'am. I mean, Lady Merida. I know you're busy." I backed toward the door, ready to run the instant I reached it.

She thrust out a bony hand as if to grab me. "Wait!"

I stopped in my tracks, too terrified to move, and stared at the hand. Blue veins stood out beneath thin white skin, the sinews from her knuckles to her wrists looked like cords, and her red fingernails were filed almost to the quick.

"You want to learn to play. You shall learn!" She pointed her index finger at the piano bench, and on legs more wooden than theirs I moved to it. She sat down beside me. "Put down your books," she said, and added scornfully, "The piano is played with *both* hands."

My hands were shaking so badly, I was sure she'd say something about them, but she didn't, and I quickly forgot my terror during the next thirty minutes as she taught me the connection between the notes on the music sheet, the keys, and my fingers. I was learning fast, I thought. Soon I would be playing like Lady Merida. Once I laughed aloud with the joy of my accomplishment and she smiled a little.

"Did you know I was a concert pianist?" she asked suddenly. She scooted me off the end of the bench and ran her fingers up and down the keyboard. Her hands no longer looked ugly but incredibly graceful. I visualized my own hands moving swiftly over the keys, imagined people around me gasping with admiration.

It started then, the kind of music that

made people walk on the other side of the road. "What am I playing?" she demanded.

Drops of sweat crept down from my hairline. Somewhere buried inside all the extra notes I recognized the tune to a song I had heard the older kids singing, but I couldn't remember the title.

"Well, what? They must teach you something at that school."

"It's something about she doesn't love him anymore," I said. "Love has . . ."

Her hands stopped in mid-air; her mouth opened with such horror that it pulled the skin even more tightly over her face.

"That," she said in a quiet, dreadful tone, "is Beethoven's great and immortal Concerto No. 5. The *Emperor* Concerto." She folded her fingers into her palms, then flung them outward. "Blackguards who write asinine tripe to masterpieces should be hanged!" She began to play with the force of her whole body. The piano seemed to be alive, to be breathing its own fury. "Bloody thieves!"

The notes swelled, vibrated, wrapped themselves around me, filled my ears, burst into the space behind my eyes.

Mrs. Limon came in quickly from another room, took my arm, and guided me toward the door. Lady Merida, although she didn't turn to look at me or slow her racing fingers, ordered, "Come back tomorrow. Same time."

The next day I learned to stretch my fingers beyond their reach. When I protested that they wouldn't spread any further, Lady Merida took my hands and showed me that they would. Then she placed my fingers on the keyboard. "Practice!" she said. "Stretch them. Practice!"

Since I didn't have anywhere else to practice playing except at Lady Merida's, she made me spend part of each lesson running up and down scales and playing the same pieces over and over. I didn't mind at first, but after two weeks of the same exercises, it seemed to me that Lady Merida should let me stop doing them.

She wouldn't. In fact, when I complained that the exercises were boring she made me practice an extra ten minutes.

But I kept going for the lessons, almost every day except for the times Mrs. Limon met me at the door and told me her mother didn't feel well.

Josie tried everything to get me to quit. I told her playing the piano was important to me and that she might as well give up.

Actually, I was tired of going so often for the lessons. I missed out on a lot of after-school talk. I especially missed standing around in the post office with Josie and the other kids, including boys, while we waited for Miss Hettie, the postmistress, to come back with the mail after meeting the afternoon train.

I had been going for the lessons for a month when I realized that I hadn't really wanted to learn to play the piano. I had wanted to make the piano sound like Lady Merida made it sound. If Josie would stop bullyragging me about going for the lessons, I could quit. I didn't think Lady Merida would mind too much. Sometimes she got a pained expression on her face when I played.

Josie didn't give up, though. She got angry every time I told her good-bye at the Limon house. And finally she said, "I'm going to get myself a new best friend."

I shrugged as if I didn't care, but the truth was that it made me feel sick all over. Josie liked to get her way, she had a quick temper, and she could be mean. But she was more fun than anybody I knew, and she always stuck up for me. There were times when I felt closer to her than to my own family. We could freely tell each other our hurts and dreams, be silly or serious, say we despised somebody without feeling guilty. But even as I told myself that all I had to do was say I wouldn't go anymore, I turned into the Limons' without a word.

Josie kept walking. I stopped before I reached the oak grove to watch her back and the way the sun seemed to set her hair aflame, and she turned around.

"I was," she said—and I heard a quiver in her voice—"going to ask you to stay all night."

"Sure," I said. "If it's all right with Mother. I'd rather spend the night with you than anything." I took a deep breath. "I'm still going for the lesson, though."

"Okay," Josie said. "Come as soon as you can."

I thought about running to hug Josie and talk with her about what we would do that night. School had let out an hour early for a teacher's meeting, and Lady Merida wouldn't be expecting me yet. But Josie had almost caught up with some other kids, so I went on up the walk.

If I hadn't told Lady Merida I would be there, I would have gone home. I had won! I had made Josie understand that my letting her be the leader didn't mean she could bullyrag me. Besides, the air had become light with spring, the sun gifted everything with lazy warmth, and taking a piano lesson inside was the last thing I wanted to do.

Before I reached the porch, I heard the piano and knew immediately that someone other than Lady Merida was playing it. This music was timid and sweet. Starting across the creaky porch, I peered through the partially opened front door. The woman sitting at the piano saw me, jumped up, and darted through the kitchen and out the back way. Mrs. Tomkin, I thought dizzily. Josie's mother! She did visit Lady Merida. She not only visited, she played the piano! She could make music! I realized that Lady Merida was watching me and closed my mouth.

"Since you're here," she said acidly, "come in."

The minute I walked into the living room, she pounced. "You're just like the rest! Insensitive! She"—she pointed a withered arm in the direction Mrs. Tomkin would be taking home through the field—

"has the soul of an artist. If she hadn't been deprived as a child, if she wasn't married to that, that ..."

"He is not either," I said, which surprised me because I never talked back to grown-ups. "Mr. Tomkin is funny—and nice." It was true. Mr. Tomkin had never ignored me like some adults did. He asked me kindly about school and my grades and my favorite subjects.

Her eyes still locked with mine, Lady Merida seemed to be asking herself a question. "Yes," she said. "Yes, I'm going to show you something."

She left the room and returned with a small, framed watercolor. It was so lovely —mountains and sky and sunlit grasses and wildflowers swaying in a breeze— that I sucked in my breath. Since, as Mother told me, I could never win at cards because my face showed everything, Lady Merida knew that I thought the watercolor was beautiful.

"Sarah Tomkin painted this from a

childhood memory of her Ozark Mountains," Lady Merida told me. "Up until now I have been the only one on this plantation who knows she has this talent —because she's been ridiculed so often."

We were silent for a minute, and when she spoke again her voice sounded squeezed out. "She can't even read. I don't try to teach her, but she's drawn to the piano like a hungry child."

Instead of giving me my lesson, Lady Merida served us tea in china cups and not-very-sweet cookies that she called biscuits. She talked on and on, sometimes growing bitter about "thieves" who stole not only music but the soul as well. She talked of her childhood, told me about concerts she had played and men who had loved her, and described how the English countryside looked in the spring.

"Meghann," Lady Merida said, and I didn't tell her Meg came from Margaret, "there's nothing wrong with playing church songs and the old familiars, but *listen* to

great music, with your senses and with
your heart, all the days of your life."

I knew what she was saying, that I
would never become a good pianist, and I
didn't think it was fair. I had done everything she had told me. Besides, it was one
thing for me to think about quitting. It
was quite another for Lady Merida to
suggest it, and I was certain she was about
to.

"You mean you want to stop teaching
me?"

She looked into her teacup, which was
almost empty, and with a strange little
smile said, "No, ducky, I don't want to
stop teaching you." She went with me to
the door, something she had never done
before. "But perhaps not so often, eh?
Say—once a week?"

I ran most of the way home, until I got a
stitch in my side, and asked Mother if I
could spend the night at Josie's. When she
said yes, I quickly did my chores, tossed
my toothbrush and nightgown and a

change of underwear into a pillowcase, and left for Josie's.

The minute I walked into her big, two-story house that had an indoor bathroom, I sensed the excitement and smelled chicken frying. I loved the commotion there, the seven children talking two and three at a time, the laughing and singing, even the arguing.

Mr. Tomkin sat in his easy chair making jokes and asking questions about school. Mrs. Tomkin, as always, moved like a phantom, constantly busy, seldom speaking. I had never really noticed her before, but now I realized that the faded hair she wore in a bun at the nape of her neck had probably once been as lush and red as Josie's. I kept looking for a chance to speak to her in private before supper, but the only time I came close, just as I was about to follow her into the pantry where she stored quarts of fruits and vegetables, Danny and James Lee, Josie's big brothers, came into the kitchen and started teasing me. Danny knelt down in front of me, took both my hands, and said, "Ah, Meggie, hurry and grow up so I can marry you." Then James Lee spun me around and said, "Pay no attention to him, darling, he's fickle. You're *my* girl." My face turned red and I hit them and wished they would keep doing it.

For supper we had fried chicken heaped high on platters at each end of the table, mashed potatoes with milk gravy, two quarts of Mrs. Tomkin's butter beans seasoned with bacon drippings and chopped onion, and watermelon rind preserves. We all said how good it was, Mr. Tomkin first.

"I would like a bit of variety, though," he said, then beamed around the table as if he had a wonderful idea. "I tell you what, let's all save our pennies and buy Mother a cookbook for Christmas."

He had always made remarks like that, and I had credited him with a fine wit, never before seeing below the surface.

Knowing as I did now that Mrs. Tomkin couldn't read, I thought that Lady Merida should have gone ahead and called him whatever bad word she'd had in mind. The kids laughed, as they always did when he said something he expected them to laugh at, but this time I understood that some of them—especially Danny and James Lee—laughed out of nervousness. They were afraid to displease Mr. Tomkin. Across from me Danny's biceps jerked after he put his hands in his lap where they wouldn't show. I knew his hands were making fists and that he would like to hit his father.

After supper I got my chance to speak alone with Mrs. Tomkin. Mr. Tomkin and the boys had gone out to slop the pigs. I had drawn scraping the dishes so I'd finished first. The girls were washing and drying and putting away. I heard Mrs. Tomkin going upstairs and quietly followed her. She had her hand on the doorknob to her and Mr. Tomkin's room when I reached the upstairs hall.

"Mrs. Tomkin," I said in a low voice, "Lady Merida showed me the watercolor you did."

She looked around like a frightened deer to see if anybody had heard.

"It's very beautiful," I said.

She blushed and a delicate smile fluttered over her lips.

"Thankee," she said.

When I went to Lady Merida's the next week, I had made up my mind to tell her I couldn't come anymore until fall. After-school softball season had started and I was trying out for sixth-grade pitcher. Josie was trying out for pitcher too, and I really wanted to beat her out. She was not as bossy anymore, but she still had a know-it-all attitude. She said she knew how to slow pitch and fast pitch and how to fake out a batter—that I didn't stand a chance.

Mrs. Limon came to the door. "Mama won't be able to give you lessons anymore, Meg," she said in a shaken voice. "She's very ill."

As I walked toward home, the gravel crunching under my shoes seemed to be saying, "She's dying, she's dying." I looked out over the flat land to where the tree line seemed to cut jagged pieces out of the sky and wondered why I was so upset. Lady Merida had never been patient with me like my teachers at school. She hadn't smiled with pride the way my parents did when I tried hard. We hadn't been friends like Josie and I were. She was not kin I was bound to love whether I liked her or not.

Still trying to figure it out, I turned onto the Blue Road and the crunching changed to a softer, sadder, earthy sound. I went down the grassy bank to the drainage ditch. Violets were growing beside the water. I picked a bouquet and wrapped their stems in a maple leaf I caught as it floated past.

All the way back to Lady Merida's I kept making up speeches, but when Mrs. Limon opened the door, all I said was, "These are for Lady Merida."

"How did you know?" she said. "Violets are her . . . her favorite."

She was going to cry. I glanced away and caught my own reflection in a window glass. My face was streaked with dust and tears.

Nothing had ever stirred the plantation up like what happened when Lady Merida died. She left her piano to Mrs. Tomkin. Not only that, but when Mr. Tomkin tried to sell it, Mrs. Tomkin told him that if he did he'd never get another meal in that house. Now people began to walk on the other side of the road when they passed the Tomkins'. I could sort of see why they did. Take the day Mrs. Tomkin told Josie and me to get our hoes and help weed the garden. She started hoeing and singing like she had a fever. She had changed her hair too. Instead of the bun at the back of her neck, now she plaited it into a crown.

Glowering at me, Josie said, "*You* might have come out all right, but she caught it—at least the crazy part. She's been like this ever since that lady passed on."

Mrs. Tomkin must have heard her, because she leaned her hoe against the garden fence and said, "Come into the house, the both of ye. I'm goin' to play my pieanna. My pie-anna," she said again, wonderingly, "what Lady Merida give me."

She marched into the house. Josie and I trailed behind her, past Mr. Tomkin, who sat forward in his easy chair and asked nervously, "What's the matter, Sarah? It come on you again? You think you better lay down and let the girls fix supper?"

"Hush up," she said.

She sat down at the piano and began to play, at first gentle and timid, like rabbits hopping, then so natural and sweet that it brought a vision of mountain flowers swaying in the wind.

"What's she playing?" Josie whispered.

Josie might have beaten me out for pitcher on the softball team, but she didn't know a thing about music.

"A concerto," I whispered back, and stood there listening with my senses and my heart while the music rose and soared out the window and climbed toward heaven.

It's the Loving
that Counts

The doors and the windows were wide open to let in the breeze. June bugs trying to get to the lamplight bumped against the screens.

The June bugs were getting on my nerves, which were not in the best condition anyway. Mother and Daddy hadn't been smiling and talking much lately, and this evening their minds seemed to be somewhere else altogether. At first I had thought they were mad at each other, but Daddy hadn't been slamming doors and Mother hadn't been scrubbing woodwork, so I didn't know what was wrong.

Daddy was sitting in his rocker by one of the lamps the June bugs were trying to get to. His shoulders were bent and his face sagged with tiredness. Every now and then he leaned over and said, "Let me see that one."

Mother and Bill and Correy and I were sitting on the floor looking through a box of photographs. We had looked at the photographs, all of them made before we moved to Arkansas, until the edges were frayed.

Ordinarily Mother spent more time with the pictures we kids were in, but tonight she quickly went to the bottom of the box. She laid aside an envelope marked, "Vera's family," and another marked, "Harth's family." The pictures she wanted to look at were the ones of her and Daddy. In some, one or the other of them was standing by their roadster, a topless car with a rumble seat.

Bill and I especially liked a snapshot taken at an ice cream social. Friends and family were laughing in the background while Mother and Daddy made the ice cream. Wearing a funny, close-fitting hat and a dress with the belt around her hips instead of her waist, Mother was sitting on the ice cream maker with her legs crossed and her knees showing. Daddy, wearing a stiff-brimmed straw sailor hat, was turning the crank—but he was looking at her knees.

Mother and Daddy looked a lot different now than they had in the pictures. Mother's face bones were sharper; Daddy's shoulders had taken on the rounded stoop that came from plowing a mule. They were older too, but there was something else, a greater difference, that wasn't as easy to put into words. In the photographs they had looked light, as if they could fly if they wanted to. Now, although they were skinnier, their bodies seemed heavy.

Mother picked up a picture taken on her and Daddy's wedding day and kept looking at it. Tears came into her eyes.

Quietly, as if he didn't want anyone to notice, Daddy got up and went into the kitchen. I followed him. He was standing over by the washstand, gazing off at nothing. I went over and stood beside him.

"What's wrong, Daddy?"

"We were married in June," he answered in an unhappy, low voice that wouldn't carry to the front room. "Saturday is our anniversary."

Everything that had happened before Daddy had lost his job in Memphis and we'd moved to Arkansas usually seemed like a dream to me, but when he mentioned their anniversary I could clearly see him and Mother, all dressed up, laughing as they went out to dine and dance and celebrate.

"I can't even buy her a present," Daddy said in the saddest voice I had ever heard.

He had bought gifts for all of us then. I remembered the time he had brought me a real china tea set. And a wagon for Bill. Correy had just been a baby but he had never lacked for toys. Now he had a rubber ball and a small red truck with one wheel missing.

There had generally been a vase of flowers sitting on the piano we had sold when we moved. And the latest record turning on the Victrola, and circuses that Daddy and Mother and Bill and I went to together. A sharp pain knifed through my heart, not so much for myself, but for all of us together, and especially for Mother and Daddy.

It wasn't bad for Bill and me here. We liked living on the plantation. There was space for adventuring. Roaming the land and the woods, we saw rabbits and squirrels, birds, and sometimes a fox or a bobcat. We had even found arrowheads left by Indians. We went fishing and berry picking and swung on wild grape vines. At school we had magic shows and vaudeville acts. Show people were mostly out of work, so they performed at schools.

It was different for Mother and Daddy.

They didn't have any fun. They only worked. And worried. I had to do something. I had to somehow make this anniversary fun and exciting for them.

I knew Daddy was right—he couldn't buy Mother a present. And he couldn't afford to take her to dinner. But he could take her out. He could take her dancing. It surely didn't cost anything to dance. He could borrow Mr. Weatherby's pickup truck like he had the time he had gone to the dentist in town. And while they were gone, Bill and Correy and I would come up with a present for them. I didn't know what yet, but I'd think of something.

"Daddy," I said, "why don't you take Mother out like you used to on your anniversary. Why don't y'all go dancing?"

He grinned lopsided like it was a sweet but impossible notion. Then he stared at me and said, "Kitten, you're right! And we grown-ups think we're the wise ones."

His face began to look like it did in the photographs—as merry as a friendly elf's.

"I'm going to take your advice and ask Mother for a date," he said.

I hugged myself for being so brilliant.

Daddy dipped water into the washpan and splashed his face, leaned down to squint into the looking glass and combed his hair. He tucked in his shirttail and rolled down his sleeves and buttoned them.

"Don't give me away when you hear a knock on the front screen," he said. He went out the kitchen door and silently closed it behind him.

Returning to the front room, I tried to keep my eyes from straying to the door, but they sideglanced. Still, I didn't see Daddy coming. It surprised me almost as much as it did the others when he tapped on the door frame. He had done a good job of slipping around the patch of lamplight that reached out on the porch.

"Harth," Mother said and glanced around.

"Daddy went out back," I told her.

Frowning, Mother said, "Strange—Brownie didn't growl."

"It must be somebody he knows," I said when Daddy knocked again.

A slight smile played on Mother's face. "I think you're right." She went to the screen, opened it, and put her hand to her throat with pretend astonishment. "Forevah more! If it isn't Harth Weston," she said.

Daddy stepped across the threshold and stood there shifting from one foot to the other like he was nervous. "My telephone's broken, Miss Vera, so I thought I—well, I came in person to ask you to do me the honor ... Miss Vera, will you go out with me Saturday afternoon?"

Mother fluttered her eyelids. "I'd be delighted," she said, then threw her arms around Daddy's neck. "You crazy Irishman."

My eyes misted. It was beginning to work already.

Daddy unwound Mother's arms. "I'm serious, hon. We haven't been anywhere together—just the two of us—for almost three years. You never get away from this plantation."

"But how ...?"

"I'll borrow Weatherby's pickup and find somebody to stay with the children."

Indignantly I said, "We don't need anybody to stay with us."

"I wanta go," Correy said.

"You can't," I told him. "It's not your anniversary. I'll take care of you, Correy."

Correy shook his head and stuck out his bottom lip. "I wanta go." Correy had had a deep voice from the time he was two, and when he got upset it went deeper.

Mother looked even more doubtful. "I don't know, Harth. We've never left the children alone and the only person I can think of to stay is Louise. It wouldn't be right. She chops cotton all week and has her laundry and housework to do on Saturday."

For the first time, Bill spoke up. "We'll be fine," he said. "If anything happens, I'll go get Aunt Louise."

It annoyed me a little that Bill was horning in on my idea. "We'll be fine," I said.

"You're outnumbered," Daddy told Mother. "Saturday at two o'clock then? Okay?"

"Yes, I guess so." Mother seemed a little dazed.

The next morning Mother opened the steamer trunk and took out her old dresses. They were wrinkled and smelled like mothballs. Daddy's suit had mothballs in the pockets.

Sighing, Mother said, "Men's clothes don't change that much, but my dresses are just not in style."

The dresses did look different from the ones the teachers wore, but I didn't want Mother to give up the anniversary celebration. Daddy would be disappointed. Also, I knew now what I was going to do for them and they would have to be away for me to do it.

"I like old fashioned dresses," I told her.

She studied a dark blue dress, laying it out on the bed.

"I like this one better," I said, holding up a black dress with a fringe on the bottom.

Mother laughed. "My Charleston dress," she said. "I can't imagine why I keep it."

I didn't want to give Daddy's and my secret away, but I had begun to worry about something. I ambled over to the dresser and took the glass stopper out of her empty perfume bottle. The stopper still smelled like rose petals. Nonchalantly, as if it were not an important question, I asked, "Did you ever go to dances in the afternoon back in the old days?"

Mother, studying the blue dress, nodded absently. "Tea dances. I loved them. You know, if I made some tucks in the waist and let out the hem ... Run get me the catalog please, Meg."

A tea dance, a tea dance, my mind sang as I danced into the front room for the catalog.

Mother opened the catalog to Ladies Dresses.

I didn't particularly like the dresses— they were neither long nor short—but the ladies had an attitude about them that made it clear that their clothes were stylish.

Mother, glancing up from the catalog, seemed surprised that I was still there. I generally spent as little time inside as possible. I liked to play outside, and I liked outside work. Except for cooking. I liked to cook, especially baking. That was why I had decided to make Mother and Daddy a cake for their anniversary.

"Do you want to help?" Mother asked.

I nodded and she gave me a pleased smile. "You can take the mothballs out of Daddy's suit pockets," she said. "Turn the pockets inside out, then put the coat on one hanger and the pants on another and hang them out to air."

I wasn't too crazy about the job. I could understand why the moths didn't bother to get into the steamer trunk. The moth-balls made my nose smart.

Mother went into the front room, sat down at her sewing machine, and started ripping out a seam.

As soon as I had hung the suit on the clothesline, I went back in. Mother had opened the sewing machine. I stood at one end of it, watching her work the treadle with her foot while she operated the balance wheel with her right hand and somehow managed to guide the material beneath the needle at the same time. I had never paid any attention before, but now that I had, it looked challenging. Maybe, I thought, I could help remake the dress.

Mother came to a stopping point and gave me another smile. "I'm glad to see you taking an interest in sewing."

I smiled back at her.

"You're not tall enough yet," Mother said. "You could run the needle through your finger. But the next time I have to fill a bobbin, you can do it."

I glanced at the machine needle and she said, "The needle doesn't operate when you're filling the bobbin. In the meantime, how about sweeping out the house." She sighed and began to sew again. "Not that it does any good."

By Friday night Mother had finished the dress and aired and pressed it and Daddy's suit. I had helped quite a bit. I had washed dishes without grumbling. I had even sung while I did them. Mother said it was the sweetest sound she'd ever heard. And I'd taken Correy for a long walk to keep him out of Mother's hair.

On Saturday, after Daddy had left for the store to get Mr. Weatherby's pickup truck, Mother went into the bedroom to get dressed. By that time I was in a tizzy. I could hardly wait for them to leave so I could start making the cake. Keeping my plan secret had been hard, but I'd decided not to tell Bill until Mother and Daddy were gone. I was afraid he would get excited and let it slip out.

Mother's cheeks were flushed and her eyes were sparkling when she came out of her room. I told her she looked prettier than the ladies in the catalog.

When Daddy returned with the truck, he told her she was more beautiful than ever.

"The dress is still too short," Mother said. "I let it out as far as it would go and it's still too short."

Daddy grinned. "Not for me, it isn't," he said.

Already wearing the suit pants and a white shirt, it only took him a few minutes to comb his hair again and put on a necktie and the suitcoat.

Bill and Correy and I went out to the footbridge and waved good-bye until the truck was far down the road. Bill and I started back to the house, but Correy stayed at the end of the footbridge, looking down the road as if he expected the truck to turn around and come back.

"I have a wonderful surprise," I told

Bill. "While Mother and Daddy are out dancing,"—I did a little jig—"we are going to make a cake for them. An anniversary cake."

Bill looked at me skeptically.

"A fancy three-layer cake. We're going to decorate it and everything."

"We've never made a cake before," Bill said. "We're probably going to make a mess and Mother will be upset."

Bill had absolutely no imagination, I thought, but I didn't say it aloud. The last time I'd told Bill he had no imagination, he'd put a grass snake in my bed to prove that he did.

Correy had finally given up on the truck coming back, and with his head down and his hands shoved in his pockets he walked glumly across the yard.

"It's time for your nap, Correy," I said. I didn't want to put up with Correy while we were making the cake. He was too little to help and would just get in the way.

"I don't wanta take a nap."

"I'm taking Mother's place while she's gone," I said. "You have to mind me. Come on in and go to bed. Right now!"

Correy's chin trembled. "I'm not sleepy right now. I don't wanta take a nap."

I grabbed his arm and he began crying and screeching, "No, no, no! I don't wanta take a nap."

If the sound carried to Aunt Louise's house, she would think I was torturing Correy. I let go of his arm and yelled, "Shut up! You hear me. Shut up!"

Bill rolled his eyes. "Taking Mother's place, huh?"

He was right. Mother never yelled. Of course, Correy didn't screech at her either.

I took a deep breath. "You may wait awhile for your nap," I said calmly and patiently. "Bill and I are going to make a cake for Mother and Daddy. You can watch if you'll be nice."

In the kitchen I put on one of Mother's bib aprons.

"Put in enough stovewood to get the oven good and hot," I directed Bill while I started setting out the mixing bowl and a sifting bowl and measuring cups and spoons. Mother didn't cook with recipes, but I had often helped her make cakes. I knew exactly what to do.

Bill frowned, but he picked up an armload of wood from behind the stove, brought it around to the front, and began laying sticks on the bedded coals.

When he had put in several sticks, I said, "That's enough. Now grease and flour the cake pans."

Bill dumped the remaining wood back behind the stove, crossed his arms over his chest, drew his eyebrows down, and glowered at me. "I don't have to mind you," he said.

"Yes, you do. I'm the oldest. I'm in charge."

"Come on, Correy," Bill said. "Let's go outside."

I did some quick thinking. Bill wasn't

being fair, but I couldn't make him do anything. Even if I hit him, he would just hit me back and go outside anyway. It would be miserable to have to do every-thing by myself.

The screen slammed behind Bill and Correy.

Quickly I went to the door and said meekly, "I'm sorry. I guess I was being a little bit bossy."

Bill and Correy came back in and let some flies in with them. I didn't yell at them. I calmly opened the door and shooed the flies back out.

Bill threw me a mean look for good measure and got down the lard can. I got the milk and four eggs and the sugar. The hardest part would be breaking the eggs on the edge of the bowl and getting them inside instead of outside, but I didn't have to worry about that yet. Mother always sifted the flour and baking powder to-gether first. And salt. A pinch of salt. I particularly remembered that because it seemed strange to put salt in a cake.

Bill leaned his elbows on the table to watch. Correy was kneeling in a chair. I had just gotten the dry ingredients measured into the sifter when Correy closed his hand around the handle.

"Give me the sifter, please, Correy," I said.

"I wanta sift."

"You're too little to sift," I said and tried to pry his fingers loose.

"I wanta sift, I wanta sift," Correy screeched and yanked the sifter hard. Some of the flour sifted out on the table. I closed my eyes and sighed. Sifting was what I had wanted to do most. But if I tried to take the sifter away from Correy, all the flour would get spilled.

Correy concentrated so hard on sifting that beads of perspiration popped out on his forehead, but he just couldn't do it. Instead of turning the handle smoothly,

he jerked it and some of the flour spilled
on the table and some spilled on the floor.
Besides, at the rate he was going it would
be tomorrow before we finished the cake.

"You can lick the spoon and the bowl
all by yourself if you'll let me sift," I told
him.

"All right," Correy said, and climbed
down from the chair.

I congratulated myself just before he
turned the chair over. "Uh-oh," he said,
and looked up at me innocently.

I didn't say a word. I didn't give him a
mean look. I just picked up the chair.

After I had sifted the flour, I thought a
prayer that I could break the eggs in the
bowl. The prayer worked except for one
egg. The one that missed plopped on the
table and the yellow broke and mixed
with the white.

"I'll wipe it up," Bill said.

He tried, then I tried. We had to keep
rinsing the dishcloth and wipinn,
and each time the egg oozed through the

dishcloth and felt slimy. My hands still smelled eggy after I washed them. "Three eggs are almost as good as four," I said.

Bill and I chased the pieces of shell that were in the bowl until we finally caught them. I brushed my sweat-damp hair out of my face with the back of my hand and beat the eggs with a spoon, then let Bill put in the milk and sugar. Bill stirred while I dumped in the flour.

Correy had climbed back up in the chair. "I wanta stir," he said.

I mopped my face with the apron. Between the oven and the sun beating on the back of the house, it had become terribly hot. I didn't know how Mother could stand working in the kitchen so much.

"I wanta stir," Correy said again.

"We're all through," I told him. But I had a feeling I was forgetting something. The vanilla! I had almost forgotten the vanilla. After I stirred in a capful of vanilla, I opened the oven door a crack and held my hand above it to check the temperature the way Mother did. Waves of heat flowed around my fingers, but since I had never checked the oven temperature before I didn't know whether it was right or not. "What do you think?" I asked Bill.

Bill held his hand above the door. "I don't know," he said. "Maybe I'd better put in some more stovewood."

"Okay. Three more pieces."

The cake mixture looked creamy and delicious when I poured it into the baking pans and slid them into the oven. I gave the bowl to Correy and he sat down on the floor. When he couldn't get anymore of the batter with the spoon, he ran his finger around the sides and the bottom of the bowl. He didn't leave a smidgen for Bill and me. Then he went to sleep—just stretched out in the middle of the floor and went sound asleep.

I swept up the flour the best I could with him lying there. I was not about to try to put him in bed and chance awakening him. Bill put the bowls and the cup and the spoons in cold water to soak. He didn't mention putting Correy in bed either.

"And now," I said, taking off my apron, "comes the best part. The bride and bridegroom."

"Aren't you going to make an icing?"

I shook my head. "I've changed my mind. I think they'll like the cake better without icing."

Bill's eyes crinkled at the corners like Daddy's did when something tickled him. "Besides, you'd have to crack some more eggs."

"Okay, smarty pants," I said. I'd not only have to break the eggs, I'd have to separate the whites from the yellows. When Mother did it, it looked easy, but after making the cake I knew it would be impossible for me.

We couldn't find a bride and bridegroom in the catalog, but we found a lady who looked something like Mother and a man that reminded us of Daddy. We cut them out, glued them to the pasteboard back of one of Bill's old tablets, and cut around them again. By then, we figured the cake would be done. I opened the oven door and peeked. The cake had risen and turned tan.

"It smells good," Bill said.

With hot pads I carefully took out the three pans and set them on the side of the stove to cool.

A puzzled line appeared on Bill's forehead. "The cake looks kind of funny," he said.

"It may *look* a little funny," I said, "but it's going to taste delicious."

To myself I admitted that there was something wrong with the cake. All three layers had the right color except for being pale, and they didn't sink in the middle, but they looked leathery. I didn't see how missing just one egg could have caused that. Probably, I decided, the oven hadn't been hot enough.

Turning the cake out on a plate would

be the trickiest part, I told Bill. I worked a
spatula around the inside of the first pan,
flipped it over quickly, and tapped the
bottom with the spatula handle.

Bill, from eye-level with the plate, said,
"You did it, Meg. It's out."

I lifted the pan and sure enough, the
cake had not broken in a single place.

"It looks better upside down," Bill said.

The other two layers came out just as
smoothly. We stacked them neatly. When
the lady and the man wobbled after Bill
stuck their feet in the cake, he propped
them up with kitchen matches.

I stood back from the cake, on the side
without the matches, and squinted. It was
not exactly what I had envisioned, but it
wasn't too bad. Actually, I decided when I
squinted a little more, it was a very pretty
cake.

Correy woke up, rubbed his eyes, and
said, "I don't wanta take a nap."

"Come look at the cake, Correy," I said.

"I don't wanta look at the cake." He

stood up and put his arms on the wall and leaned his head on them. "And I don't wanta take a nap. I told you—I don't wanta take a nap." He kicked the wall, then sat down and squalled because he had hurt his bare toes. In his whole life, Correy had never behaved as badly as he had today.

"If you were my kid," I told him, "I'd take a switch to you."

He made an ugly face at me, pulling the skin under his eyes down with his fingers and sticking his tongue out. I couldn't help it; I pinched him. He really squalled then.

"Come on, Correy," Bill said. "We're going outside."

I didn't know whether Bill was mad at me or not, and I didn't care.

By time time it was 3:45, and I expected Mother and Daddy to drive up any minute. I tried to read my *Black Beauty* book, but my mind kept straying. The day hadn't gone the way I'd planned it. Bill hadn't let me be in charge. Making the cake had been hot, hard work. Correy had been impossible. But Mother and Daddy were having fun. They had to be to stay away so long. I imagined them whirling around the dance floor, Mother laughing, Daddy smiling tenderly down at her.

And there was still the cake. The grand finale to their anniversary celebration. Every time I went to check the clock, I stopped to admire the cake.

The minutes crawled by with all the speed of a lazy inchworm. I was beginning to worry that Mother and Daddy had had a wreck when Bill came running inside to tell me they were coming. It was 4:32.

The three of us and Brownie waited by the footbridge while Daddy pulled the pickup to the side of the road. Before Mother reached the footbridge, Correy, with his arms outstretched, ran to her. She cuddled and kissed him.

"Could you still dance good?" I asked as we started across the yard.

Mother looked blank.

Daddy started to laugh, but he evidently saw the expression on my face because he suddenly stopped. "I'm sorry, honey," he said. "I didn't realize that you actually thought we were going dancing."

"But, oh," Mother sighed, "we had a wonderful time. We went to department stores, we had a Coke at the drugstore—and we watched the people."

They had watched people?! What kind of celebration was that? All afternoon I had been picturing them dancing, and they had just been watching people. It was like expecting a peppermint stick and getting a biscuit instead. It was worse. It was like thinking there was a beautiful horse in your yard and it turned out to be a homely mule. I was so let down I could have bawled. Now there was only the cake to make this anniversary special.

As we stepped inside, Correy said, "We have a s'prise."

He had been awful and now he was

happy and about to ruin everything anyway.

Correy looked at me and put his hand over his mouth. I could tell that he was sorry he had almost given away the surprise. It was hard to believe that only a little while ago he had been making ugly faces at me.

"Close your eyes," I told Mother and Daddy.

Bill and I took their hands and led them to the kitchen.

"You can open them," I said, and Bill and I did a leap and presented the cake with a sweep of our hands. "Ta-da."

"Oh, Harth," Mother said softly, "look what our children did for us."

She brought in saucers, and a knife to cut the cake with. Daddy poured glasses of milk. When we were ready, Mother removed the lady and man cutouts. "I want to keep them," she said.

Slowly, as if she were sawing through wood, Mother cut the cake. She kept smiling. One by one she put wedges of cake on the saucers and each one made a thump.

Before I took the first bite I knew the cake was a disaster. I chewed and chewed and chewed. I swallowed. Even Brownie would scorn this cake—and Brownie loved cake.

Numbly, I stared down at my saucer. From start to finish, my plans for Mother and Daddy's anniversary had been a failure.

"How much butter did you put in, Meg?" Mother asked. "I think that's the only thing wrong—that you didn't put in quite enough butter."

I dropped my face into my hands so they wouldn't see the dumb tears. I hadn't put in any butter. I had gotten the flour and baking powder and milk and eggs and sugar right. I had even remembered the salt and vanilla. But I had forgotten all about butter.

"Meg, darling, it doesn't matter," Mother said in such a warm positive voice that I stopped crying and lifted my head. "It's the loving that counts." As I looked at them, I realized that Mother and Daddy were glowing—they looked as happy as they had in the photographs.

"It's not so bad if you crumble it up in your milk," Bill said.

"I don't see anything wrong with it," Correy said.

"It's a fine cake," Daddy said. "Just the kind we need. People's teeth don't get enough exercise nowadays."

The windows were wide open. The wonderful sounds of June—birds singing, chickens clucking, Dolly's new calf bleating—floated in with the breeze and mingled with our laughter.

Dust Devils

With a length of sawed-off broom handle, Josie swung at a big bumblebee. She missed, which was unusual for Josie. "It's too hot to knock down bumblebees," she said. "It's too hot to do anything." She came up on the porch with Grace and me.

Josie and Grace had come to my house to play, but I couldn't think of anything to do. As Mother said, the sweltering weather might be good for the cotton, but it was certainly miserable for people. I stretched out on my stomach, daydreaming that I was lying in a pool of cool water, drinking lemonade with chunks of ice in it.

Grace, who had been holding one end of the thread tied around a bumblebee, let it go. I watched the string trail behind it as it flew away. Knocking the bees down stunned them long enough to get a string tied around them, but we didn't bother to knock them down again and untie it when we were tired of playing with them.

Grace leaned back against the wall, picked up the Sears and Roebuck catalog we had brought out with us, and flipped it open. We knew the catalog by heart so she didn't have to search long to find the page she wanted.

"Look at them," she said. "Don't they look cool now?"

I propped my chin on my hands so I could see. A full page of ladies wearing nothing but their step-ins and brassieres smiled at us.

"When my family went fishing in the Mississippi River," I told Grace and Josie, "we stayed all night on a sandbar and I

went swimming in my underpants. No top. Just my underpants."

Their mouths dropped open and Josie's freckled face turned almost as red as her hair.

"Of course, I was just nine years old."

"Oh, well," Josie said, "that's different. You can do a lot of things when you're nine that you can't do when you're almost twelve."

Josie was four months older than I and she constantly lorded it over me. Grace was older than either of us—thirteen—but she didn't mention it.

Grace had flipped over to another section of the catalog, but she kept her hand where the ladies in the step-ins were. On the page she turned to, men in suits and neckties were all smiling too.

"Now this city slicker," Grace said, pointing to one with perfect teeth and perfect hair, "has his eyes on this girl." She pointed to a lady in her underwear whose teeth and hair were every bit as

perfect as his. "But he better watch out"—
she turned a bunch of pages at once—
"'cause this is that girl's daddy, and he
plain don't like city slickers." There, grinning evilly, stood a man with a shotgun.

I giggled, but Josie yawned and scratched
a mosquito bite on her arm. "I'm about to
burn up," she said.

"We could go stick our heads under the
pump and take turns pumping water on
each other," I suggested.

Josie scratched her ankle. "I have a
better idea. Let's go wade in the canal."

Mother didn't like for Bill and me to go
to the canal, not even to fish. There were
deep holes in it, and turtles and snakes. I
would have to fib to her, say we were
going to Josie's or to Viola's school to play
on the flying jenny or something, and I
didn't like to do that.

"I know a nice, shallow place with a
sandy bottom," Josie said. "It's up close to
the highway."

I pretended to be studying the pictures

of boys and girls in their fine clothes as Grace idly turned the pages of the catalog. "That's a long way," I said. "Besides, I don't think Grace can go."

Without looking up, Grace said, "Mama and Daddy would as leave I don't come back until nightfall. They told us kids to go somewhere because they couldn't stand the fussing and the heat both."

I had wondered why Grace was in such a talkative mood. Now I knew. She felt free.

"My daddy hates lay-by because he gets stuck at home with all the young'uns." Grace's lips curved in a faint smile. "I'm for it. Let's go."

I thought about Grace's father. When he punished her, he whipped her with a razor strop. Even if he *had* told her to get out of the house, I didn't know whether that included wading in the canal.

"You really want to go, Grace?"

"She told you she did," Josie said.

I waited for Grace to answer.

"Yes," she said, "I do. I can't see nothing wrong with it."

I chewed my thumbnail and came up with another argument. "Y'all don't have your shoes and overalls." Daddy had made a strict rule that Bill and I were never to go into the fields or the woods or on the ditchbanks without wearing shoes and overalls. There were too many snakes and poisonous insects.

"Oh, for Pete's sake, Meg," Josie said. "Don't be such a worry wart. We'll just be extra careful."

"I'll go ask Mother," I told them, getting up slowly in the hope that they would change their minds. By the time I went through the screen, though, I had changed mine. I would just ask if we could go for a walk. I wouldn't say where we were walking to. I didn't know why I hadn't thought of doing that before. Of course, that meant I couldn't put on my overalls and shoes either. That would give it away.

Mother was reading in the front room.

She had a fan in her right hand and sometimes she would fan herself and sometimes lean over to fan Correy, who was asleep on a quilt on the floor. He lay all sprawled out, his white-blond hair damp, sweat beading on his nose. Poor little thing, I thought.

"Mother."

She was so engrossed in one of her old books, *Drums*, by James Boyd, that she jumped. Mother said that every time she read a book again she got to know the people better, so she became more involved in their lives.

"Is it okay if Grace and Josie and I go for a walk?"

"It's too hot to go for a walk."

I sighed the same way Josie had and said, "It's too hot to do anything."

Her finger marking the line where she had stopped reading, Mother said, "All right, Meg. Don't stay away too long." She picked up the fly swatter by her chair and slapped a fly that had crawled onto

Correy's quilt. "It's unbearable," she said, kind of waved the fly swatter for me to go, and started reading again.

I put on my straw hat and went back outside. Josie and Grace picked up their hats too. We were afraid we would bake our brains without sunhats.

Gray dust covered our bare feet as we walked down the road to the canal, then cut across the end of the cotton rows. The cotton bolls were opening and fluffy white cotton was bursting through. Soon it would be ready to pick, and lay-by would be over.

Now and then we had to dodge dust devils that sprang up in front of us. The dust devils, which only came during hot, dry summertime, whirled crazily for a minute, then disappeared.

Although the afternoon sun was behind us, Josie's face was so flushed from the heat that her freckles had a greenish cast. Grace didn't look as hot as Josie, and she didn't have to worry about blistering like

Josie and I did because she had tanned to a pecan brown. We were all wearing cotton dresses, but Grace's had been made from a washed out flour sack and hung loose. Sometimes she picked up its hem and fanned herself with it. She had on pink bloomers.

"This is where we cross over," Josie finally said. "It's a secret path."

"I'm surprised your mama let you come," Grace said as we started to climb the high mound of dirt that had years before been scooped out to make the canal. "Especially without making you put on your shoes and overalls."

I caught hold of a vine to help pull myself up. "I didn't tell her where we were going," I said, a little proud of my foolery. "I just asked if we could go for a walk."

"You lied," Grace said solemnly.

"She did not!" Josie flared.

It was the same as at school. Josie took up for me before I could defend myself.

"We did go for a walk," Josie said.

"I heard a preacher talk on it once," Grace insisted. "He said there are two kinds of lies. Lies of omission and lies of commission. And that one is as bad as the other."

Deciding it best not to take sides, I didn't say anything. I would have liked to agree with Josie, except what Grace said seemed right. I kind of wished I had asked Mother if we could go wading in the canal. She would have said no and I would have pouted and told Josie and Grace what an unreasonable Mother I had, and I wouldn't have to worry that later my conscience would act up. But my budding regret vanished like a burst soap bubble when we topped the mound and saw the canal dancing its way toward the river.

We reached the bottom of the mound, crossed the grassy shelf, and picked our way down the steep bank through saplings and weeds, watchful for poison oak and snakes. Blue runners and king snakes didn't worry us, but water moccasins, which were as at home on land as in the water, did. A moccasin could pump enough poison into your veins with one strike to lay you out cold dead before you'd taken twenty steps. They were as vicious as mad dogs and didn't have to be threatened to come after you.

"It looks so good," I said when we reached the water's edge. "This was a wonderful idea, Josie."

Josie bowed and her hat fell off. Grace balled up the front of her dress and stepped into the clear water. She waded up and down and Josie and I waded in too. Compared to the air, the water, fed more at this time of year by underground springs than by rain runoff, was so cold that goosepimples popped out on my arms. It didn't last long though; the sun kept bearing down on the rest of me.

"Let's go swimming," Josie said.

"In our clothes?!" I didn't say what I was thinking; Grace said it for both of us.

"You've gone plumb crazy, Josie Tomkin."

"Not in our clothes," Josie said. She looked around and whispered, "Let's go swimming naked."

Grace scrambled to the bank. "Now I know you've gone crazy. The heat's got to you. I'm going home."

Josie waded out after her. "Come on, Grace. There's nobody to see us. Who'd ever know?"

I had already peeled off my dress.

Grace kept looking around to reassure herself that nobody was watching us. "Well," she said, and I knew she was about to say, "okay," but she changed her mind again and shook her head. "Y'all would see me. I don't let nobody see me naked."

"We won't look, Grace," I told her, folding my dress and underpants. I laid them at the base of a maple sapling and jumped in. Josie came right behind me.

Shivering with the coolness and the excitement, we waded out to the middle where the water came all the way up to our shoulders. We could see our toes on the bottom of the canal. Josie and I splashed each other and laughed and dog-paddled among the ditch weeds. A perch swam out from one of the weed patches and we tried to catch him.

Wearing her worried-old-lady face, Grace swept her eyes up and down the canal, trying to see around the bends, probing every nook and bog and bush. "All right," she said. "Don't look." She turned her back while she pulled her dress over her head. She stepped out of her bloomers, first one leg and then the other, laid them close to the water, and slid in backward.

"I'm starting to get a bosom too," Josie said. "I don't know why you're so shy about it."

"You looked!" Grace screeched.

The three of us were sitting in the water talking, far enough out so that it came up to our chins, when I saw him. A man was walking toward us along the top of the high mound. He was coming from the direction of the Blue Road, just as we had, with the sun at his back. My voice box had locked itself, so I grabbed Josie's arm and squeezed. She and Grace turned their heads and saw him at the same time. Grace made a little sobbing sound. I jumped up, ran to the bank and to the maple sapling, which provided scarce cover, and got into my clothes faster than I had gotten out of them. Josie did the same thing, but she slipped and fell when she was trying to put her underpants on.

The man had disappeared down the other side of the mound.

"Do you think he saw us?" I asked Josie.

"Sure he did. He's going to pop back over straight across from us. We'll have to take the shelf home or we'll run smack into him. Grace, for Pete's sake, come out of there! Come on!"

Grace was still in the water. Only her head was on the bank. She had pulled her bloomers over her head.

We had to take Grace's arms and yank before we could get her to come out. Her teeth were chattering. "Who—who was it?"

"I don't know," I said. "We couldn't see his face. He had on overalls and a sunhat."

"It was my daddy," she wailed. "He looks just like that."

"A lot of men wear overalls and a sunhat," Josie snapped at her. "Grace, will you hold your arms up? Please. We can't get your dress on if you keep letting them flop."

With Grace clothed and calmed down, we started up the bank. Josie and Grace were ahead of me, following the same secret path we had taken down. I kept looking up at the top of the high mound, expecting the man to pop over as Josie had predicted he would, got off the path, and stumbled on the roots of a tree that had been felled during wilderness days. When I glanced down I was looking right into the cat eyes of a coiled moccasin. The thick part of his dull gray body was as

big as my thigh. The scream in my brain came out a strangled croak, but it was enough to make Josie and Grace look back.

"Run, Meg!" Josie yelled. "Run!"

I couldn't run. My feet had grown into the ground. My heart was choking me. I was looking right at the snake's fangs and the cottony lining of his mouth.

From the corner of my eye, I saw Josie, brandishing a stick, charging toward me, and her movement gave power to my feet. I leaped and scrambled frantically upward and heard the moccasin strike the bank where my bare legs had been.

We ran along the shelf until the Blue Road bridge came into view. My knees buckled then and I dropped. I sat hunched over, sobbing and shaking. Josie kept patting me and Grace fanned me with her sunhat.

When my sobbing had subsided, Grace said, "I bet he didn't miss you by no more'n a frog's hair."

I nodded, drawing in a shuddering

breath and appreciating more than ever before the wonder of being alive.

"The next kid might not be as lucky as you were, Meg," Josie said. "I hope that man we saw finds the snake and kills him."

"But ... but what if he doesn't?" I asked.

I knew from Josie's expression that she wished she hadn't thought about the possibility of the snake biting somebody else. "Sure he will," she said emphatically. "Men are always on the lookout for moccasins."

"Maybe," I said, "we should tell our fathers." I saw fear cross Grace's face and added quickly, "I mean, Josie and I should." Grace's father might not care if she went wading, but he'd sure care about the swimming naked part.

"No!" Josie said. "We can't tell anybody! We couldn't see who the man was, so I don't think he knew who we were either. But if we tell about the snake, they'll put it together. *They will know.*"

Grace was hanging her head and plucking blades of grass. "Josie's right," she said weakly. "We can't tell nobody."

I knew they had a point. Most everybody on the plantation, including my parents, did a lot of putting things together and figuring out the answers. "Okay, I won't tell Daddy about the snake," I said, but without much enthusiasm.

Josie narrowed her eyes at me. "You've got to swear, Meg."

I didn't want my parents to know any more than they did that we had gone swimming naked, but she had gone too far. Like always, she'd brought out my stubborn streak.

"I don't like to swear and I'm not going to," I said.

Josie jumped up. "Some friend you are!"

She had done it. She had made me mad. I jumped up too and stuck my chin out at her. "Well, that goes both ways!"

"Come on, y'all," Grace said tiredly.

"Let's go. Meg's not a tattle-tale, Josie. You know that."

"Sometimes," I said, "Josie doesn't seem to remember anything. I've never told on her in my life. Not even when the principal threatened to expel all the girls if we didn't tell who climbed through the boys' bathroom window one night—and wrote, 'Hi, Jeff,' on the floor with lipstick."

"Meg," Josie shot back, "can't even remember twenty minutes ago! That snake would have bitten her sure if I hadn't yelled. And gone running with a stick to save her!"

"Baloney! It was probably you and your stick that made the snake mad."

Grace put her hands over her ears. "I don't want to hear no more. It's sinful for friends to say such mean things to each other."

At the Blue Road Grace said good-bye and turned toward her house. When Josie and I, walking on opposite sides of the road, reached my house, she didn't say a word or even slow down. I hated her until I opened the front door. Then I pushed our quarrel to the back of my mind. We had a fight about every two months anyway. Considering the heat and what had happened, it was no wonder we'd had this one. I'd tell her that when I went to her house next week.

Bill had gotten home from wherever he had been playing, and he and Mother were in the kitchen snapping beans for supper. Correy was eating a raw bean.

"Have fun?" Mother asked.

"Yes, Ma'am," I said, and took some beans to snap.

Mother's face puckered with concern. "Meg, is anything wrong?"

"No, Ma'am," I said, and snapped the bean I had picked up into tiny pieces. Now I had lied with commission as well as omission. My head started to hurt.

I couldn't eat much supper, and after I went to bed, I lay staring at the ceiling.

The more I thought about it, the worse going in swimming naked seemed to be. If they found out, Mother and Daddy probably would be so ashamed of me they wouldn't be able to look at me.

But what if the man hadn't found the snake? What if nobody found him? I pictured a little boy going down to the water and disturbing the moccasin. The faceless kid changed to Bill. He was lying on the bank gasping out his last words, "I've ... been ... snakebit." Brownie had his head lying on Bill's chest. It seemed so real that I started to cry. Finally, I drifted into a fitful sleep.

When morning came, I couldn't get up. "I'm sick," I told Mother.

"Do you hurt anywhere?"

"Mostly my head hurts. But I feel bad all over."

She held her palm to my face. "You don't seem to have a fever," she said. "Would you like some breakfast?"

I shook my head. "I'm not hungry."

After she left I drowsed until Daddy came in and laid a wet, cold cloth on my forehead. "How's my girl?" he asked.

"Okay," I mumbled. He didn't know it, but he almost didn't have a girl. I wanted to tell him then about the snake, but I had promised Josie and Grace I wouldn't.

Daddy sat down on the side of the bed. "I think I have just the medicine to make you well," he said. "I pulled a watermelon early this morning while the dew was still on it. It's in the pump house keeping cool."

He was being so sweet. He knew how much I liked watermelon. And I didn't deserve it. His little girl that he was so proud of had done something awful, had gone swimming naked.

I closed my eyes and turned over on my side with my back to him so he wouldn't see the tears squeezing out from beneath my eyelids.

Daddy stood up and said, "Meg...," then gave a sigh and left.

Mother came back and brought me some weak tea. "I wish we had ice to put in it," she said.

I drank a little of the tea and gave the glass back to her, sinking down on my pillow.

She took my hand and asked gently, "Meg, what happened yesterday?" and the tears that had been burning under my eyelids finally had to come out.

"I lied to you," I sobbed. "We didn't just go for a walk. We—we went swimming naked in the canal."

She didn't say anything, and when I gathered up enough courage to look at her, she was smiling. "Now I have a confession," she said. "When I was about your age my sisters and I went swimming naked in a creek."

I stared open-mouthed at her. I couldn't believe she had ever done anything like that.

"We never did tell our mother, so you did better than I." She smoothed back my hair. "I'm sure she knew, though—just like I did."

I sat up. "You knew?"

"At the store yesterday afternoon—Daddy was there playing checkers—a man told about seeing three girls swimming naked in the canal. Never mind who. He only saw that you were girls and turned around in the hope that you hadn't spotted him and spoiled your fun. It wasn't hard to figure out who the three girls were. There are little scratches all over your body, Meg. From ditch weeds, I expect."

I slid my gown up and looked at my legs. Sure enough, there were thin scratches on them and I knew they would be on the rest of me too.

"Did you tell Daddy?"

Mother nodded.

My headache went completely away. I knew Mother and Daddy wouldn't mention who the other girls were when I explained that Grace and Josie might get in trouble. And I didn't have to keep my promise anymore because they already knew about swimming naked. I could tell Daddy about the snake now and stop worrying about Bill getting bitten.

"Is Daddy—ashamed of me?"

"Well," Mother said, lifting an eyebrow, "he did ask if I thought I could make you a swimming suit."